TATTOO

D. Thomas Gochenour

Copyright © D. Thomas Gochenour, 2017. All rights reserved

978-1-387-27312-6

The euphoric high started as usual.

Blue and warm yellow lights danced around his room. He felt a sexual tingle, maybe even an erection, but above all, a sensation that something warm and soft was embracing him, tickling him. His temples throbbed but without any pain, his breathing was easy and rapid but deep. It seemed like he was gulping in fresh mountain air, but otherwise, he felt the warmth. The blood racing through his limbs, causing his eyes to flutter. Something in his eyes caused them to refract the light into vibrating horizontal panels and put the room around him out of focus and crystalline, shimmering outside of the usual color scheme for the room. At one moment he jumped up from his arm chair and his feet danced wildly. At the next moment he was in the chair again—it didn't seem to fit him-- writhing with pleasure or tapping both feet, beating the arms of the shabby chair. He felt happy and one moment was standing on the ceiling and the next twirling. Visions of girls laughing with him, other girls swimming naked in the surf off Venice Beach, flames of bright bonfires leaping into the early evening sky, his brother hugging him and carrying him across a river just as when he was six years old, his 7th grade teacher gently stroking his head while telling the class that he was a champion writer. He sang, then rushed over to his CD player and put on some Kenny Rogers music and sang yet louder. He went to his door and stepped out onto the balcony and began howling like a dog and then singing. The

night was clear and pellucid, and bright. Its warmth embraced him like a lover's hug, caressing his hair and his back. He had sensations of lightness, sometimes feeling that he was flying around the room or above the balcony. It was all so timeless and happy.

But the time did pass and slowly and gently but steadily the ecstasy began to wane, became less intense, the soft warm lights and pastel colors dimmed. The visions of beautiful, lithe naked women who desired him and laughed at him evaporated. The tender caresses he felt ceased. Slowly, he began to have more regular corporeal sensations, weight, fatigue, straining muscles, chill. But still his eyes saw the world through refracted lines, unfocused, vibrating. He had no idea how many hours had passed since the height of his euphoria to when he became aware of creatures creeping up his legs, under his skin. Little creatures which seemed like beetles with serrated carapaces were creeping up from the floor from his feet under his skin. They made little mounds in his bare legs looking like nothing so much as tumorous lumps in his veins. After marching up his legs, causing Jack more and more alarm, he could feel this procession moving around his crotch and up in the area of his lower abdomen. At the same time, the lights began to waver between bright yellow and a smoky, unclear dimness. The creepy almost itchy sensation he had on his abdomen caused a short panic attack in Jack. He tore off his tee shirt (blue with the Grateful Dead's smiling skeleton). And it was at this time that his first tattoo came to life. Or that his dark visions began of this tattoo coming to life.

It was a large tattoo on his right shoulder that Jack had gotten not many months before from the "Weedhead", tattoo artist John Garcia, the master at the Weed Shack. It was one of the things that Jack was most proud of. A tattoo of a flag draped coffin, surrounded by exploding bombs and Humvees and battle standards which was a freely rendered memory of the sight Jack had had at his brother's funeral after his body had been brought back from Afghanistan. Weedhead had listened carefully to Jack describing the scene at the military cemetery and had improvised this tattoo using his special red and bright blue inks for the American flag and creating the background scenes from what he thought war in Afghanistan might have looked like. Weedhead had never himself gone to war instead he had been a protestor against the war in Vietnam, but he embellished the tattoo with images from the TV coverage of the wars in Vietnam, Kuwait, Iraq and Afghanistan that flooded his pothead imagination. Jack had asked Weedhead to paint this tattoo as a memorial to his brother Bobby who had been killed in a bomb explosion on the road outside Kabul four years earlier while Jack was serving in the army in Iraq. He had all his life admired and looked up to his older brother, the successful brother, and the news of his death had devastated him. That is why he had wanted the tattoo put on his shoulder so he would always remember him.

On this particular night coming down from his cocaine high, Jack jumped up and ran to the mirror to look at

the tattoo on his rather thin and bony right shoulder and upper part of his pecs. He was still seeing the world in black and blue refracted lines. The world around him was beginning to look like the dark lines of a manga murder story. He could see in the mirror the crawling subcutaneous lumps were advancing toward the tattoo—their steps were beginning to feel irritating to him and he itched over much of his torso. And then in front of his reflected gaze at his tattoo the flag on the coffin was ripped off and the heavy cover of the coffin thrown aside, revealing the body of Bobby in his dress military uniform. The body stood up in the coffin and slowly painfully stepped out, even though it had only one leg and one arm with jacket cuff and the pants cuff both pinned up and dangling loosely. Bobby's face was not expressive, cold and lifeless looking. It was a zombie. And then Bobby walked right out of the tattoo and down onto the floor, This vision of a zombie walked away from Jack, limping awkwardly, it moved out of the apartment and out the door onto the balcony and into the night's dark air. It seemed the room was spinning around Jack's head. Fear was tearing down the walls around him, his furniture was bumping about on the floor like a frozen steak on an over-hot griddle, unpleasant clanging noises were coming at him from all directions. He saw pieces of the room and furniture expanding and then contracting in his eyes like some out of order zoom effect. And then the beetle-like lumps on Jack's torso one after another jumped out of the coffin on his shoulder tattoo. They took on the form of dark skinned, blank faced lifeless men dressed in

rags hanging loosely from their limbs. More zombies! But they did not hang around. One after the other they followed Bobby's limping body out the door into the now howling night air. Zombies everywhere, they were taking over, Jack thought not so lucidly. In all eight black zombies tumbled out of Jack's tattoo and into the night. Jack made no effort to stop them, he was too much in shock and his feet now seemed cemented to the linoleum floor, even though his furniture continued to tap-dance around the room and the sofa and table were puffed up and twice their usual size. "Zombies will eat the world", he thought, "I have to do something. I have to stop them." He rushed to his small chest of drawers and pulled out a Smith & Wesson pistol. He grabbed his shirt and put it back on as he rushed out of the room onto the balcony in front of his entry door. Looking around he did not at first see the zombies shuffling away out of the parking lot but he did finally see them under the glow of a street light at the far end of the parking lot in front of the apartment block. He ran over to the staircase, his head throbbing. It seemed as if he was shouting, but he couldn't tell as all his senses were so scrambled. His feet slid down the metal stairs as if he was skiing down them and then he too rushed off into the deep dark night air.

Jack woke up the next morning draped over the living room sofa, his head still throbbing in pain, the shirt lying on the floor, and his mouth dry and gummy, dried saliva dribbled down his chin. He was intensely thirsty

and he got up with some difficulty to look for some water. As he stumbled to the kitchen to drink from the faucet, he noticed his Smith & Wesson lying in the middle of the main table. He thought that was strange: why would his pistol be lying out in the open there? After he had a long drink and rinsed his face in the kitchen sink, he then felt very hungry. He looked in the fridge but there was nothing there except for some spoiled butter, a half full bottle of ketchup, and a leftover piece of dried old pizza in a cardboard box which he had bought a week before. Damn he muttered. He'd have to get a Subway sandwich on his way to work. He looked in his pocket and pulled out $3.80. Was that enough even for a sub? Maybe he could afford a six inch sub sandwich. He put some water on the stove to boil and took out a small bottle of instant coffee. There was enough for a few more cups of coffee, but only one teaspoon of sugar remained in the bowl. He could have used a coke breakfast but he had no more lines. And he had spent all his money on last night's batch. He walked back into the main room picked up his pistol and, again wondering how and when it got on the table, he put it away in its usual place. He went into his bedroom which was cluttered and from a pile of clothes sitting on a chair, he pulled out some dirty overalls and long sleeved shirt.

He then left for work, stopping at the Subway near his garage and he gobbled down a six inch sandwich. It would be his meal for the day. He pulled up to Pancho's Garage, Auto Service and Body Shop late. Hernandez, the owner and son of the eponymous

Pancho, was waiting for him impatiently at the garage door. "You're late again Jack. We've got a backup in the body shop as you know." Jack did not answer at first. "You haven't given me the estimate for the body work on Browney's Lexus yet." Hernandez spoke with a typical low pitched Mexican-Angeleno accent of the the Chicano communities of Los Angeles, an accent that was easy to make imitate and make fun of which Jack did at every occasion. "I told you, Panchito, (his name was Jose) that car is not a simple body job. The frame is bent something awful. I can replace the broken body parts, but it still will run improperly. The insurance company won't pay for it. Tell Browney that it is obvious that he didn't bump into a tree. Maybe he fell at speed over a high curb stone before hitting a wall or another car. We can't fix the bent frame, so no estimate for the rest of body work." "You tell him, Jack" (he said it like Iyack). "And besides I'm working most nights on the other cars. You don't pay me no overtime to be here until after nine o'fuckin' clock." "Browney's not going to like it. He's a tough one and big honcho in this neighborhood." "Yeah, yeah. So I'm afraid of a low life nigger rapper." He said it in the way that Browney himself would have said it. "You're no good Jack. Always trouble with you. Always late." Jack went to his work bench inside the still cool garage. "I still have two cars waiting on the paint shop." He shouted out at Hernandez who had already walked away. 'Shit,' he thought, 'that Panchito is really pushing it. Who does he think he is? Uppity spic.'. He

was angry, because now he could not hit Hernandez up for an advance on his bi-weekly pay check. He needed cash soon, before Friday, because now he didn't have any more and no way to get any money in the next two days. Again he had shot off his lip. Like his dad had always said: Keep your lip shut or you'll find yourself in deeper trouble. Jack had always followed that advice when he was in the army, but here in LA with all the Chicanos and niggers running around it was sometimes hard to keep his lip zipped.

He pulled on a work smock and went to the jobs clip board. Nothing had moved overnight so he picked up where he had left a bumped and scraped Ford the day before. His left shoulder almost immediately began to feel sore. The wound lay underneath the blue red and grey tattoo of Bobby's coffin, the tattoo that was meant to hide the scar. Sometimes it would get real sore inside, like it had been those first days in the hospital in Afghanistan, a burning pain that rose in the joint and came up through the scar, even though the bullet hadn't hit his shoulder joint. He remembered that day, a rare day when he was sitting as a spotter on top of a troop carrier rushing to the site of a IED bombing just south of the capital when suddenly he felt a hard shove and a dull burning sensation in his left shoulder, not strong enough to knock him off his perch. It had to be a stray bullet or a bullet from a really distant sniper because the bullet went straight through his shoulder only chipping a little bit of bone off his shoulder blade where it stopped. If it had been only a little farther it would have hit major arteries or even smashed into his face

and then he would have come home in a body bag, like his brother. The doctor who treated him said that he had been very lucky, but Jack, who was a sharp shooter of great talent, knew that he was saved only by distance. The shooter that day was probably more than a mile and a half away and he could not have been shooting to hit him, he was only shooting in the general direction of his Humvee. He had not been so lucky as to get a Purple Heart and immediate discharge either. He was back on his rotation, patrol duties and mechanic duties, in only two and a half months. The doctor had told him that he would only have that scar and no lingering pain or dysfunction in the shoulder. But he had been wrong. He had occasional pain and soreness, like his grandfather's acute arthritis, on and off ever since. The tattoo hid the scar, but did not cover up the intense intermittent soreness. Eventually as he was discharged Jack did get a Purple Heart for his very real wound. He hung it up when he got back home on the wall in the family living room next to Bobby's. There was nothing Jack could do about the pain, so he had always just put up with the occasional pain and tried to carry stoically on. It was Weedhead who suggested that the proposed tattoo could cover up the scar so that no would ever see it on the beach for instance or in bed. He got out his grinder and turned to grinding a sidebar on an old Pontiac that he had been working on for several days already. After an hour, he went to the coffee machine and poured himself a cup, added milk and stood for a moment under a television. At that

moment there was a newscast and he listened in as the morning talking head began her routine. "This is the latest news on the shootings last night in South Central Los Angeles. Police report that there were six or seven shootings in the West Century Boulevard section near Inglewood last night. Six men were shot from behind at close range by an unknown assailant. Four of the victims were killed and the other two are in critical condition in hospital. The shootings took place between two and four o'clock this morning—in an area which is normally quiet and where there are rarely people walking outside at that time of night. These could have been drive-by shootings but we just don't know yet. We are told that all six of the victims were African-American men, but one may be a dark skinned Latino. There were no witnesses and at the time no one heard or reported the shots. Only one of the survivors thinks he saw a man run away from him and climb into a dark late model Chevy pickup. The men were found several hours after the shootings by passers-by who called the police. Police are saying that the shooter used a high powered hand gun. Traffic is closed on many of those streets in the Century Boulevard 96th street area. The police are asking residents in the neighborhoods between 94th and 104th street if they heard or saw anything suspicious last night to come forward and report to them what they heard. They are asking citizens to report any missing relatives since last night. All of the victims were young men in their twenties or thirties; five did not have any identification." 'Probably because they were peddling

drugs or weed,' thought Jack. "The identities of the survivors and the slain men are being held up until the victims' families can be contacted. The police have no motives in these shootings and do not believe that any of the victims are related. We will report more as any further details become available." Jack listened carefully to the entire news item but did not react. 'Must've been gang war executions.' He thought. Afterwards he finished his coffee and returned to the Pontiac, taking a glance at his dark blue Dodge pickup parked outside by the bay doors of the body shop. A few hours later the paint shop man, named Pablo, came by to pick up one of the cars ready for painting. He was a lazy, fat Mexican who spoke rarely because he was an illegal and because he knew almost no English and Jack had the hardest time getting him to finish paint jobs on time. No amount of shouting or cussing at him moved this Pablo to work any faster. "There's another one waiting here for you." he shouted at Pablo with contempt, "It's been waiting here for you for more than a week already." Jack thought again of asking Hernandez for some money in advance but he let it go after he ate two stale doughnuts that were on the coffee table in the grimy lunch room next to the engine repair and tuning shop.

Jack got through the rest of the week by pawning his pistol the next day. He got $90 for it and thought he should buy some food and gas for his truck before he squandered it all away on drugs. He wanted to redeem

the gun but he could not think when he could afford to repay the loan. Sometime soon he thought. He didn't expect to get his salary from Hernandez until Saturday and he'd be very hungry by then. Maybe he would go to Weedhead on the weekend and get a new tattoo. Maybe he'd go to the rifle range in Orange County and do some target shooting. He liked shooting and was doing it less and less in the past two years since he had moved to LA. But until he could go, after work over the next two evenings Jack stayed at home and played his favorite wargame on his computer. He especially liked one called Shooter where there was some reasonable verisimilitude to actually sniping with a high powered rifle and it was set in an animated world that looked a lot like it had in Afghanistan. He'd spend three or four hours online on the game, each time trying to increase his score. Sometimes he'd eat a Subway sandwich while he was playing online game, but usually his only dinner was a frozen pizza and a cup of coffee. From the moment when his pa first took him shooting when he was eight, Jack had always like rifle shooting. And he was good at it. Better than Bobby had ever been. At target shooting Jack always scored more killing shots than Bobby, and on hunts, he usually bagged the wild pig or white tailed deer while Bobby just shot up the trees or scored a wounding shot when the animal ran away. When he was fourteen, his pa gave him his own rifle, a Winchester 30.06, which Jack treasured and took on many hunting trips throughout high school and which he only stopped using after he bought himself a Marlin 336. Jack's sharpshooting was

about the only thing that his pa had acknowledged as something that Jack did well. Most of the time pa was critical of everything Jack did. But he was a really good shooter. That one time when the three of them went on a hunting trip down in Alabama, Jack had killed three bucks: Three shots, three kills. Bobby had only clipped one deer. His father on that day was effusive in his praise. After that trip Bobby always acknowledged that Jack was a better shot. After Jack signed up for Afghanistan and started training he was almost immediately assigned for specialist training and quickly became a designated marksman, and by the time his unit had shipped out to combat duty it was clear he was going to be a key member of a fire team platoon. Some of his commanders he tried to convince him to become a sniper, but Jack let that slide. He wasn't interested in the complete isolation and long hours of being a lone sniper on a dusty roof in some hostile Afghan town. But like a sniper after he started applying his marksmanship, he kept track of the number of "kills" he had during his two year tour, before he was hit. When on combat missions when confronted by fire fights, Jack would calmly take his shooting post and float into a quiet reverie as he aimed his M-14, completely losing awareness of his platoon mates unless they kicked him and told him to move. They would tease him and call him "Dreamer" because he was so concentrated on the targets at the end of his sight. He never saw the people he killed as people. They were mere targets, dressed in loose garb and

funny mops on their heads, a little like deer with antler racks. It didn't bother him that he shot and killed real people. From the first to the fourteenth, they were all little more than lifeless moving targets to Jack, and his focus was always on making a killing shot on these targets the first time. He never followed up his kills to look at the slain Afghan up close, to see where his shot penetrated. That just did not interest him. When he had gone hunting, he always would track down his kill, inspect the accuracy of his shot, and of course harvest his dead animal as a trophy. While he was still living in Tennessee Jack would regularly go hunting, usually with his father, often as much as twice a month during the season. But after he had moved out to LA he went hunting much less often. The legal hunting grounds were far to the east, often in desert terrain. But on occasion he went hunting by himself. And very early on he even went hunting in the San Bernardino mountains in the National Forest, even though hunting there was prohibited. He was not very successful on his hunts,--the deer were few and the bear very reclusive and in all his time hunting the mountains to the east of LA he never saw a puma, although there was clear evidence of them. Besides even getting to those mountains was also a long drive and took effort, and he had to be careful not to get caught by wardens. Even though there was a very limited hunting season up in the mountains around the national forest, Jack never bought a state hunting license, so he was always in violation of the hunting laws. When that next weekend finally came, Jack drove out early to the shooting club,

took his rifle, and went up into the mountains above Riverside to try some hunting. He spent most of that day driving back and forth on the sparsely used mountain roads leading into and out of the national forest around San Jacinto Mountain. He didn't get in any shooting that day, but still he got back to his apartment very late at night after tramping through miles of chaparral and dry forest without spotting any deer. The forests in southern California were so much different and less fecund than those he had grown up with in Tennessee and Alabama. He was refreshed by the hunt and felt elated even after he went back to the garage the next day.

He left work earlier than usual one evening and finally got around to visiting Weedhead again not long afterwards. The little nondescript shop was located in a strip mall on a main cross thoroughfare. Its front wall was glass but it had been painted shades of black and blue so that no one could look in from outside. Jack was struck immediately as he stepped in with waves of the sweet-acrid smell of marijuana: Weedhead had gotten the name from smoking copious volumes of the marijuana and the shop was completed saturated from the smoking. Weedhead said he smoked so much of it that he no longer had hallucinations but instead he got inspirations and it steadied his hands. Weedhead was a sight: he had an unkempt beard which crept over his lips and into his mouth every time he tried to speak so that he often sent small bits of spittle flying whenever

he did speak and then when he did his voice always sounded mumbled. His head was covered with a vast mountain of uncombed hair, mostly slate colored but also flecked with white, so that he looked like a weed garden. This was exceptional, as most of the tattoo artists Jack had seen before had shaved their heads completely bald and had tattoos over their cranium. Weedhead's arms, neck, and chest however were completely filled in by blue, orange and black intersecting tattoos. He wore a sleeveless undershirt and frayed blue jeans. His tattooed feet showed through as he was wearing only pink plastic flip-flops. The shop was cluttered. It was divided into three small work cubicles with screens giving the client privacy while getting a tattoo. Every surface of the shop and the cubicles was covered with sample tattoos on thin paper, on clothe, or photos, but as they were nearly all black ink they gave the shop a gloomy, oppressive cavelike atmosphere as if the visitor suddenly fell out of the sunny skies outside down into an underground cell. Jack had been there twice before and gotten two tattoos, but Weedhead did not recognize him. "Hey man. What's happening? Need a tattoo today or do you just want to smoke some weed, chew some fat, and hang out?" Jack did not hang out and he did not enjoy just sitting around talking. "I thought maybe I'd get another tattoo." "So what'll have? We have a big selection. How much do you want spend?" "I only want to spend two hours this time. I was thinking of something military." Jack had gotten his first tattoo just after he had signed up for the army. While he was still in high

school, while there were some kids who were beginning to get tattoos, the school authorities banned the display of tattoos, that is they couldn't been displayed and they had to be covered by clothes. Also Jack's father would have given him another beating if he had gotten a tattoo while he still lived at home. Jack didn't need that at the time. His father beat him often enough anyway. So he got his first tattoo in a grimy little tattoo shop next to the Waffle House on the highway from Camp Benning going into Columbus, Georgia. It was a small tattoo of a heart with a dagger through it and a U.S. Army banner around it. He now thought it was ridiculous and glad it was hidden most of the time. Weedhead was bouncing his head and muttering, "cool, cool. Do you mean like army emblems and US flags, tanks and helmets, or are you a Nazi type? Want something like moto gangs? You can look over on this wall for different military images. I haven't had any soldiers come here in a long time, are you a veteran?" "I was in Afghanistan fighting with the 10th Mountain brigade. My brother died fighting in Iraq with the Marines. That was the image of the tattoo I got here last time." And he pulled aside his shirt to show Weedhead the tattoo of the coffin. "Ah now I remember. I guess you do look kinda familiar." Jack looked over the pages of tattoo choices and chose one, a pair of crossed M4 rifles, like the ones he had used in Afghanistan. "Oh okay, so you're a shooter, eh?" "Put it on my right upper arm." "That's not bad. It should take me less than two hours to do. Got the time?" They agreed and Jack went into

one of the cubicles and took off his shirt. It was his military service camouflage shirt with its embroidered nametag on it. Weedhead set out his needles and ink—he only needed black—and then put on hot pink latex gloves and was ready to begin. Not long after he started the pricking, he started making small talk. “So you were in Afghanistan. During Bush’s surge? How many people did you murder? I didn’t go to Nam. I was opposed to it. Unjust killing and murdering of those Asian gooks, even if they were communists. It wasn’t right. I couldn’t do it. And Uncle Sam shouldn’t have done it. Ya know what I mean?” Jack thought Weedhead gabbed like a barber, and he did not want to answer because it would make Weedhead talk even more. But he couldn’t let go the hostile question. “I didn’t murder anyone. I was there in the conduct of war.” “Fine, but it was an unjust invasion of a poor developing country.” “They attacked us first, Muslim terrorists. Or perhaps you didn’t notice the Twin Towers’ collapse?” “Yeah, yeah. Sure I noticed. But we did not need to invade that country and shoot up so many innocent men, women and children. So did you kill any Afghans?” “Yeah, sure I did. Taliban fighters. If I hadn’t shot them they would have killed us, either by bombs or ambush fire.” As soon as Jack said that he almost choked because he knew that he had seldom killed any Taliban fighters. He had probably “dusted” (as the saying went) mainly civilians or poor non-committal peasants caught between the Taliban and the allied forces. Weedhead began inking, and he kept on gabbing. Even though the needle pricks were

uncomfortable, Jack was discomfited more by Weedhead's constant banter, probing. "I can't imagine what it's like to kill a man with a rifle. I mean that seems so strange to me." "It's easy. A lot easier than with a knife or with your bare hands." "Oh I guess so. But I wouldn't know that either. I've noticed all the video games are about shooting and killing. Personally I like Super Mario, but the other games seem to always take the perspective of a rifleman blasting away at anything that moves. But if you're a shooter, who's killed, I can be cool." Jack thought, it's not very cool to be a blabbermouth like you are. Maybe he would talk less if he had a reefer to smoke. At that very moment, Weedhead asked Jack if he minded if he lit up a reefer. "No please." Weedhead put his needle down and pulled a joint already rolled out of a drawer, lighted it and took a deep draft. "Want one?" "No thanks, not now." Weedhead had been the man in LA who had given Jack the connections to the marijuana and cocaine distributors. He continued with the tattoo. After a few moments, he asked Jack, "So is it easy to kill people? I mean, no bad feelings or revulsion? No regrets? Do you feel guilty?" Jack had never thought about it so bluntly. "I don't reckon so. No different than killing an animal that you're hunting, a deer, or a pig, or a dog in the street." "I mean, like you know, a human being is a moral creature." "You say so. I'm not so sure that it makes a difference." "So, would you shoot and kill a friend, the same as a dog?" "I don't have any friends." That seemed to silence Weedhead for a moment. He

again put down his needle and took a deep draft, looking up at the ceiling. “Do you have some impulse to kill people, like you do to kill animals that you hunt?” Jack again did not expect this question, nor know how to answer it. After a while, he just said, “Sure I do.” He paused a moment, looked at Weedhead’s floppy hair, then looked away. “Just like those people who have road rage on the freeways here. They want to kill people. And only have regrets when they get caught after they’ve shot and killed a few, and tied up traffic.” Weedhead finished his reefer and then the tattoo. He seemed calmer. “That’ll be $37 for the tattoo.” And when Weedhead took the money at the cash register he again asked. “Hey dude, isn’t that guy, Jose, the comics artist, isn’t he your friend?” Jack pulled on his shirt. “I don’t see much of him at all, so I can’t say he is my friend. We both served in the same unit in Afghanistan.” “Cool. Next time, I can propose to you a really good tattoo –a work of real art. But it’ll take some time to do. Okay?” “Yeah sure”. Jack could not imagine then when a next time would be.

Jack’s thoughts flashed over the time he had first met Jose Gonzales in their shared barracks near Kabul in Afghanistan. Jack had noticed that on most evenings, Jose would stay in the barracks at a table by himself busy with a pencil and a piece of paper. When Jack first moved over to see what Jose was doing, he first noticed that Jose appeared to be drawing cartoon figures, but that when Jose became aware of Jack looking at him, he stopped drawing, grabbed his paper up and hid it under his arms. Jack had never served in a

platoon with Jose so he introduced himself and then rare for Jack he asked Jose what he had been doing. Jose said simply drawing some stuff. Jack continued to let his curiosity push him forward. "What are you drawing? It seems you're drawing most every evening. I've seen you." Jose, who was very reticent and shy, showed him the piece of paper. "Marvel comics!" whispered Jack out loud. "No," said Jose, "my characters, not Marvel's." Jose had a strong accent. "I draw only my own characters for superhero comics." "But that is really good. It looks like Captain America or something like him." Jose looked at Jack with a distrustful almost contemptuous gaze. "No, I mean you draw really good. Just like in the Marvel comics. Can I watch you?" Jose consented and continued drawing his superhero, and in the weeks after that Jack would sit by Jose's side watching as Jose drew out of his imagination, one character after another. Neither Jack nor Jose would say very much, and Jose never much inquired about Jack. In their day jobs, they remained in separate platoons and in separate patrols out and around Kabul and its vast region. On some evenings either Jose or Jack would not get back to the barracks for one or two nights at a time. Once Jack asked Jose if he had put together a story with his characters, on another occasion he asked if Jose wanted to work for the comics or video companies. Jose had said yes, he very much wanted to be a cartoonist for some video graphics firm, after he was finished in Afghanistan. He had even put together a portfolio of cartoons that he could submit.

Jack then asked him if he could make cartoon characters of the Taliban fighters who they confronted every day, and then of the grunts that were fighting in their unit, the 10th Mountaineers. Jose thought that was a terrific idea and for the next three months his sketches and cartoons moved from over-muscled superheroes in skin tight costumes, to over-muscled GI grunts shooting up tall, evil looking Taliban figures with exaggerated kohl-lined eyes and big long noses and large black turbans draped over their heads. "And this one is you, Jack." said Jose as he showed him a lean heroic looking soldier. "His face kinda looks like mine, but he's too tall. That figure looks more like my brother, Bobby. But he's a marine." Not long after that, Jose moved to a less comfortable Chooville camp in another city and Jack kept in touch with him by military phone until he was sent home. Jose left him his contact info when he shipped out. And that was how Jack had come to LA.

That all finally came about because of another fight with his father. After his discharge, Jack had gone back to working at his father's filling station, garage and service station on highway 6 on the outskirts of Murphysville. It was about a year after Bobby had been killed by an IED in Iraq and about six months after Jack had come back. The army command had not let Jack fly back stateside for Bobby's funeral at the time. When he did come back, he decided he would continue working as a mechanic with at his father's garage just as he had through high school and at the same time he would take courses at the Cumberland

community college so he could get his mechanic's accreditation. He was nearly finished with the courses and was getting ready for the test. His father had continued to express his criticism of nearly everything that Jack did, both at home and at his garage. Nothing he could do was good enough. And he had expressed his skepticism about Jack's ability to pass the accreditation exam at the college on a number of occasions. And at work, his father treated Jack like a servant, shouting at him, criticizing him, and sometimes even delaying his salary, which was not good to start with, only about $11 an hour. In the almost ten months after Jack had come home from war, they did not go hunting or shooting together. Father said that without Bobby, he just did not feel like going out hunting. Then one evening after dinner, the two of them were sitting on the sofa watching a baseball game when Jack's father blurted out, "That could be Bobby pitching this game. He was much better than this son of a bitch pitching now." Jack did not reply. He had tried to play baseball in high school on the team where Bobby was the All-State pitcher. He had tried but he never quite made the cut. After his graduation, Bobby had won a scholarship at the University of Tennessee to play baseball. There he continued pitching and hitting at prolific rates, so that even pro scouts were monitoring him. Then in his third year at university, Bobby had suddenly quit the team, took leave from the university, and signed up with the marines to go fight in Iraq. "Why that fool left a promising career to go off

and fight someone else's fight, I'll never understand." Jack still made no comment, because he did not understand that move either. He and Bobby had never talked about their decisions to sign up for the wars in Iraq and Afghanistan. "Maybe it was patriotism." He muttered. That had certainly been one of Jack's reasons for signing up with the army only a few months after his graduation from high school and only two months before Bobby made his decision to join the marines. He had always been trying to emulate Bobby whom father saw as a true talent and hero. Jack had not discussed his decision with Bobby in advance of signing up, but he had told him as soon as he had. Jack had signed up impulsively in a sudden spurt of patriotism in response to a program he had seen about the surge that President Bush had ordered. And he had signed up so that his father would see him as a hero for a change, independently of whatever Bobby was doing. "Nuts to that." His father bitterly muttered. Jack saw his father's stern face, staring hard at the TV screen. Maybe he detected that his eyes were beginning to tear up. "If you'd been more dedicated to your job in the body shop, maybe you would have put the armor on his vehicle and Bobby would still be living." Jack protested, "How many times have I told you that putting armor on the Humvees was not my job? And that in any case I was in Afghanistan and he was in Iraq. I was patching up vehicles in Afghanistan, usually after they hit IEDs." It didn't matter. Father was blaming Jack for Bobby's death, for Bobby's decision to sign up with the marines, for his decision to

throw away his promising baseball career. Bobby had been quite happy and proud to be a marine fighting in Iraq. He found the work satisfying and exhilarating. But he died suddenly and without warning when an IED tore through the unarmored vehicle he was riding in near Falluja. It was such a big blast that it tore the vehicle in half and blew four pieces of Bobby's body more than twenty yards away, along with the bodies of his three other mates. Nothing Jack had said before or after then would change his father's mind. Father was sure Jack was involved by his negligence, even if it was the negligence of the Department of Defense. "You were never any good, Jack. And you know that you sent Bobby off to war. If you hadn't joined up, he wouldn't have gone." Jack jumped up shouting. "Why can't I get it through your thick head? I had nothing to do with Bobby's death. I want him here as much as you do. You can go to hell." And he rushed out of the room. That was the moment Jack decided he had to move away from home, get away from his father. The sooner the better. The next day, Jack remembered Jose and that he lived in Los Angeles. He called Jose at the contact number he had left him. After several attempts when he got no answer, he finally got Jose on the line. Jose had found a job doing just what he said he had wanted to do, drawing cartoon characters for video game sites and so he could only answer his phone in the evenings. They decided that Jack should come to LA. It would be easy to find a mechanic's job and Jack could stay at Jose's place until he found a place of his

own. Jack made his arrangements. He packed up his truck and waited to tell his father of his departure only on the evening when he received his last paycheck. He had already told ma, but swore her to secrecy until he had the chance to tell father himself. When he told father that he would not be coming in the next day, he thought father would hit him. He stepped back in anticipation of a blow to the head, but he hadn't needed to. His father glowered at him with anger and contempt in his eyes, but he did not hit out at Jack. Nor did he say anything.

Jack left home early the next morning and began his drive to LA in his dark blue Ram pick-up. He stopped three times staying in a Motel 6 along the interstate. The drive out to LA through Oklahoma and Texas as monotonous and boring as it was still surprised Jack. As he moved steadily westward, the landscape became brighter, drier and barer then what he was accustomed to in Tennessee. By the time he crossed Arizona and into eastern California, he thought the landscape and the brilliant skies, the arid, rocky mountains and the sparse forests, and scruffy undergrowth reminded him of large parts of Afghanistan. It wasn't until he climbed over the San Bernardino Mountains and caught his first sight of the Los Angeles basin and the Pacific Ocean beyond that he realized that LA was a desert city sitting on the seaside. He couldn't at that time see much of the city as its infamous smog sat over the main part of the city like a dusty white blanket. As he came into the eastern reaches of the city, he was reminded of entering Kabul on a dust storm day. But even after

arriving in the city, he thought that arrival was hard to realize. The city was an endless sprawl of very similar looking, lifeless dirt or sand colored buildings. It took him hours of stop and go driving, checking the navigator, and standing at traffic lights, before he found Jose's house. Jose was not in when he arrived and pulled into a short concrete driveway. He called Jose's cell phone, but again got no answer and left a message. He waited in the heat and stuffiness the rest of the afternoon just outside Jose's small, one story cracker box house which stood on a street with no trees or shade anywhere. As the evening light began to soften into gray and a cool breeze slowly refreshed the air, Jose finally called him back on his cell phone. "Sorry Jack, I didn't call back sooner. Are you now in LA? Are you going to stay tonight at my place?" "Yeah, hey Jose, I'm at your house, at the address you gave me. I've been waiting here for several hours. Is there any place nearby where I can get a drink and grab something to eat?" Jose told him of a mini-market a few blocks distant. They agreed to meet after two hours. When Jose finally drove up it was just getting dark. Their reunion was strained and awkward. Both young men were shy and reticent by nature, they found it hard to even look each other in the face. Jose seemed familiar to Jack, but in civilian clothes he looked small and different from the seated cartoonist those many evenings in the barracks. For the first time Jack saw that Jose was short, and pudgy. They did not have much to say to each other, after they shook hands, a

strange silence halted them. Finally Jose motioned Jack to enter his house. Jack picked up a large duffel bag from his truck and went inside. He stayed as a guest in Jose's house for about three weeks. In that whole time they barely spoke more than a couple hours together. And at that their conversations were limited to the brief evening hours when Jose was there and then they spoke only for Jose to instruct Jack on how to conduct life in LA, how to find an apartment, where to get a tattoo, where in the city the auto shops were located, a recommended night club, where to watch out for gangs. They never ate together, mainly because their schedules never coincided. In the evenings after Jose returned from work, Jack would often spend the remainder of the evening playing video war game on his computer and Jose would watch television or go out for dinner. Jack slept on the pull-out sofa in the main room in front of the TV. After Jack found a rental place and moved out they hardly spoke together again, except rarely and briefly on the phone. LA was that way, people or friends could disappear from your life by moving to another part of the city eight or ten miles away. But Jose was a LA native and the tips and recommendations he gave Jack served him well in the first couple years that Jack lived there. Like the recommendation to go to Weedhead. Or his introduction to Hernandez. When Jack moved out of his apartment, Jose thought briefly about whether even liked Jack very much. He felt there was an underground stream of anger and violence in Jack, that he was a dormant volcano waiting to blow up. But after only a moment's thought Jose decided that it

did not matter. There was no camaraderie between them. As he turned to do other things, Jose merely felt some relief that thereafter he would not see Jack again, just as he would not see again any of the other platoon mates he had sat anonymously with for nearly two years. And that was for the better.

Hernandez had hired Jack at once when he learned that he was not only an experienced mechanic but had done body work in Afghanistan (although Jack had actually been doing that for only a few months). He offered to pay him more than what his father had been paying him, and he would give him overtime also, depending on the work load. Once he had gotten the job at Hernandez's, in eastern LA, that set up and accelerated his search for an apartment. He moved into his own place about two miles from the garage less than a month after he had left Murpheysville. He furnished it simply and even after he had lived there for five years, it was sparsely furnished, a few chairs, an oval table where he used his laptop computer, a settee and a double bed. It was enough. He spent only a few waking hours there on any given day. It was mainly a place where he slept, sometimes ate, and often played video war games for a couple hours each evening. Most of his free time, most weekends, he was out.

He did not seek out a Baptist church so Sundays he was always free. While he was growing up and in the family, he had always gotten dressed up and gone to

church with his entire family—it was at the United Baptist Church on Second Street in downtown Murpheysville. The people were nice there, his father excepted, but Jack did not participate or socialize much at all with the other Baptist kids. So often while he was a teenager, he, Bobby, and father would go out shooting after church service, but get back home in time for Sunday dinner which was served in midafternoon. But he gave up church attendance as soon as he left for Camp Benning. All he could remember about Sundays at the Baptist Church was sitting next to his mother who was apparently wearing a sweet smelling perfume which bothered his nose, or all the times his father was shouting at him to get dressed so they could leave for church on time, or occasionally boxing his ears, or the one time when he was eleven, when his father reached over around mother in the pew and swatted him so hard on the side of his head for not singing a hymn that he nearly had cried there in the church. He had felt so ashamed at the time, but later it was memory that kindled only rancor. It had been at about that time that Jack's father began to occasionally beat him.

Throughout his teen years Jack's father would occasionally give him a beating with his fists. It was different than the times when he was younger when he would punish him with a swipe of his belt. He started beating him in anger, striking out at his second son who shamed him, at about the same time that he began to beat his wife, Jack's mother. Jack never understood the connection clearly. He was eleven when one day he was sent home from school early for fighting at play

period. When he got home he noticed that there was a delivery van parked on the street out front. He entered the house and thought it was empty. But then as he was walking to his bedroom, he heard was sounded like squeaking floor boards from their parents' bedroom. The door was opened so he peeped in and saw a sight which he did not recognize at first. There was a naked woman sitting on the bed on top of some man. It was his mother of course, but her back was half turned toward his view and he had never seen his mother naked before, so at first he did not recognize what was going on between these two strange adults in his parents' room. She was bouncing up and down violently on top of the man, and their heaving and movements were what caused the bed to groan and squeal. He saw her full breasts flapping up and down and he stared at them. He had stood and watched, transfixed for what seemed like twenty minutes but was of course much less. He had an involuntary erection, although otherwise he stood frozen. After their humping climaxed and slowed down, the man became aware of Jack's presence and his reaction caused his mother to look back and see Jack. She jumped up off the bed in alarm trying to cover her breasts with one hand and her vulva with the other. "Get out. Close the door." She hissed as she ran into the bathroom. She looked just like the full chested nude models he had seen in the *Playboy* magazines he had carefully studied at the house of one of his school friends. Jack had immediately retreated and the door was slammed shut.

He was also struck by some strange aroma, some perfume his mother was wearing. It was a sickening sweet smell which seemed familiar. Sometime later he was trying to impress Bobby that he was the holder of an important secret, which of course Bobby spent every effort to coax out of him. Apparently then when he had told him the secret, Bobby told their father about this terrible sin—the son viewing the mother's sex, not so much the terrible sin of their mother's adultery. And after that Jack's father beat him. He didn't beat Bobby. Jack never saw his father beat Bobby. But on days when father had a troubled countenance on his face or was chewing his lips, he often would haul off and hit Jack once or twice with his fist in his face or shoulder or stomach. Jack at first always cried, not so much from the blows but from the clear sense of his somehow being at fault, or of receiving such a clear signal of his father's disapprobation. As he grew older and taller, Jack became more used to the beatings, but nothing prepared him for the beating he got when he was sixteen, almost seventeen. He was already working almost every afternoon at his father's garage, he had his own car and driver's license, and he had already realized that he could not match his brother's athletic success in football or baseball. One evening when he was about seventeen and Bobby had already gone off to university, he came home from the garage and saw his father beating mother and he intervened to try and stop him. But father at that time was in a rage, shouting obscenities at her, calling her a whore and public disgrace. When Jack tried to stop the beating, his father

turned his rage onto him and beat him up, knocking him to the ground, kicking him and pounding him with his fists. All Jack could do that time was curl up and try and protect his head. He ended up with a chipped tooth, two black eyes, and bruises on his back and legs. He could never forgive his father after that and he never forgot the pain and intense fury that had fallen on him that evening. He didn't go hunting or shooting with his father ever again. He could not tolerate his father's company, and deep inside he feared he might on impulse shoot his father if they were close together and a loaded gun was in Jack's hands. Later Jack would find himself suddenly feeling huge waves of anger washing over him for no particular reason and he would feel a strong impulse to hit someone. Occasionally he did strike out, but at school this only got him in trouble. He was suspended once in his junior year for hitting at a classmate who was giving him lip. It was concluded that he had been provoked, but Jack knew better. He would have hit out at anyone on that day, and he was perhaps fortunate that he only stuck another aggressive young man or he could have hit some unfortunate victim completely out of the blue. His father continued to beat Jack's mother too from time to time. One evening, Jack came home as his mother was stepping out the door a barrage of cursing and shouting was raining down on her from inside the house. She was dressed up, even had on lipstick. "Where are you going, ma?" "I'm going out with the girls. Will be back late. Dad is furious that I'm going out, so keep

your head low." And it was then that Jack again noticed the strong aroma of that familiar perfume he had smelled on her so many times. "What is that perfume, you're wearing?" "It lavender, lo de lavender. Your dad's favorite." And she rushed to her car and drove off. Jack followed her advice and avoiding his father, he went back out to a fast food stand for dinner.

Early on in his stay in LA, Jack looked up on the internet a shooting and gun club and found one located in the hills of northern Orange County which was not too far from his apartment. He drove over there one Sunday morning—it took a little more than an hour--and he joined. From then on he made this shooting club his Sunday morning routine in place of church attendance although he rarely went there more than twice in a month. When he did go he would spend several hours at the club, which was very simple and rustic with several outdoor ranges spread over the acres of the arid hillsides. The club also had a range for skeet shooting and two indoor ranges one for pistol target shooting and another for Olympic target shooting with rifles. He left his hunting rifle in a locker there and it was from other members at the club that he got tips on where best to go hunting in the region. Everyone recommended the mountains in San Bernardino and Riverside counties, about another hour distant. He struck up a kind of camaraderie with one of the shooters at the club, a fast talking man named Kyle, a native Californian who was about thirty or thirty five years old and also a military veteran. Once they even talked about going hunting together. But Kyle would only go

hunting for mule deer in the very restricted hunting season and only with a legit hunting license. Jack said he didn't have a license and couldn't be bothered getting one. So Kyle then backed out on that occasion. The fines if you got caught were too high for him and he wouldn't go. So another time some months later Kyle proposed that they go hunting on a shooting farm in Riverside County where they stocked javelinas and feral pigs, a bit like the hog hunting ranges in Alabama. Kyle was not a particularly good shot, but Jack killed three razorback hogs. He didn't especially like it: it was like hooking trout in a barrel. As Jack saw it the only advantage of hunting on a shooting farm was that they had a butcher at the farm house who would cut up your kill. Kyle took nearly all of the meat. Kyle was most helpful in recommending to Jack a number of places to go to in the mountains where the hunting was usually good. And he showed him on the map how to get to those places. But over his first several years living in LA, Jack did not see Kyle often, and then only when both went to the shooting club at the same time on the weekends, and then not by arrangement.

In the first six months after he started working at Hernandez's garage, Jack set up the routine that he would follow over the following five years. His life was occupied nearly entirely by his work at the garage, first as a mechanic and then more and more as a body repair man with only occasional engine repair work. He kept to himself and did not talk much at all with the

other mechanics at the garage, all of whom were either young Chicanos--Mexican Americans or emigrants from Mexico or El Salvador. The other workers spoke amongst each other entirely in Spanish—even if they knew English well enough-- and only when they had to tell Jack something they would speak with him in often broken English. Some of them, the newer emigrants, spoke no English at all. Jack made no effort to learn any Spanish. He felt that as they were living in the United States they should be speaking English and he resented it that they didn't. Occasionally this caused some friction when he couldn't tell them the parts that he was looking for, because they didn't know the names in English and he didn't know the names in Spanish. He concluded that they were deliberately not speaking English to him as a way of making him look bad, and sometimes he was sure that they were mocking him too. Over his first year working there Jack noticed that the other mechanics did not gang up on him as a group because there was such a high turnover among them. Some would work for several weeks and then disappear inexplicably, others would say they had to leave for family reasons and then would never come back. Hernandez was quick to replace them. The clients of the garage were mostly English speakers, even when they were Chicanos, so in some cases Jack had to be the client interface. He then had to convey instructions to the other mechanics some of whom understood him perfectly and others who didn't understand anything that Jack said. To this language obstacle it was clear to Jack that many of his work mates did not actually have

a very good technical training or background and they did not always know what to do or how to diagnose problems. This was another reason why Jack tended to work by himself, and why he preferred body repair work because he was able to work by himself in a separate bay. But he still had to remain involved in engine repair whenever spare parts had to be ordered from a supplier. The work itself constantly changed. There was still the constant search for the mysterious sound or squeak, the usual tune-ups or search for why engine performance had suddenly plunged, but so many jobs were different that it remained interesting and not routine. With body work, the tasks were always different. Along with the usual dents and banged up fenders, there were smashed doors, caved in roofs, folded hoods. He was surprised however after he had worked only a few months in the body shop when he got his first repair job where the car had been shot up and had bullet holes all along one side. In the coming years he worked on a number of these kinds of jobs. Many of these jobs, were not paid for by insurance coverage. Hernandez had a lot of regular clients, like Browney, who came to him for urgent repairs or patch up jobs and who paid in cash, no insurance payments, no questions asked. Hernandez suggested to Jack that they were the cars of some of the local gangs or racketeers. Many of these clients wanted to preserve or maintain cars that they had had specially altered or had given a distinctive paint job or had painted with favorite symbols or badges. These cars were their totems and

could not be easily replaced. They had to be restored even when repair and restoration might cost more than buying a new car. Jack came to understand this. One of the oddest jobs he got was a car that looked like it had been peppered by golf balls, its top surfaces pocked and dimpled, but the sides were untouched by these dimples. In Tennessee such a car would be junked, but this car had on its sides paintings and decals with all kinds of gang symbols. This car had in fact been hit by a downpour of big hailstones. After his first year working at Pancho's garage, he got a body job that really impressed him. It was a silver Mercedes which had been tail-ended. On the hood of this car was a painting of a nude woman who was reclined, her legs somewhat spread, she was arching backwards her face looking as if she were in the throes of passion, writhing in pleasure, or as if she had just finished making love with the viewer. Jack loved this painting and for a long time stared at this beautiful woman and her accurately portrayed features, her broad hips, her vulva, her closed eyes, her shoulder which seemed to be quaking and her breasts were flattened like round foot cushions because she was on her back. The artist had used tints and shadowing which suggested that the woman was dark skinned, although his portrayal of her head hair and pubic hair suggested that the woman was not. Jack was so impressed that after a long examination of the painting and before he started working on this car he got his camera phone out and took a picture of this painting. He took several photos in fact, some from different angles.

Jack spent long hours at the garage and most often returned home late in the evening. Once home he would reheat some leftover meal or put a frozen pizza or a TV dinner in the oven to heat. And then on most evenings he would then get on his computer, looking briefly at the news and then getting onto one of his war video games. He rarely ever went out in the evening. It was in his first year in LA that he also began searching pornography sites. He would end his day by looking at some of these sites, and often would end the night by masturbating and then falling directly asleep. The morning routine was to wash and shave, have breakfast of some toast and coffee, clean up the dishes. He was paid by Panchito fortnightly in cash so at the beginning of that pay period he ate well, doing food shopping on his way home from the garage, and by the end of the fortnight he ate at scraps. Jose had recommended to him that Weedhead was the best tattoo artist, especially if he wanted a Transformers tattoo. So early on one late evening he went to Weedhead's and got his first tattoo from him—the crossed M4s. He also got a recommendation of where to go to buy weed or other euphoric drugs. From a man named Manuel. So one Friday evening, just before the end of twilight, he drove over to a street that meandered along the Los Angeles River embankment in an industrial zone. He stopped and walked across the street to a parked, unmarked black Chevy. A Mexican with a thick black moustache was sitting at the wheel. "Manuel? Jack asked through the open window. The man nodded and signaled for

Jack to get in the front seat. There was another Mexican young man sitting in the back seat. They drove slowly off. "So what do you want, Gringo?" "Weedhead said you have marijuana. But what do you recommend?" "We have weed, good stuff too. Came in today. We also have coke and crack. You got enough money, we sell you good stuff, no bunk. Fresh from Mexico today." "Don't know what I want. How much does coke cost?" The Mexican parked the car not far from where they had started and looked closely at Jack." He chuckled, "So you're new at this? You know how to use it?" he asked mockingly. "Sure, I'll snort it." "What's your name Gringo?" "Jack, eh, Jack McGee." He didn't think of giving the Mexican a false name. "So I'll tell you what, I'll give you a gram and you'll give me a Franklin. Then you'll get out of the car and walk back to your pick-up and I don't see you again. Okay?" Jack nodded. The man in the back gave Jack a polyethylene sandwich bag with a little bit of white powder in it and took the bill from Jack over his shoulder. "Hey,baby man, don't o.d. on your first use." And Jack got out and walked off into the already dark night. It wasn't his first use-that had occurred just as he was re-patriated by the army but just before he was discharged a little over a year and a half earlier at a disco joint just off base in South Carolina. He and some mates had gone into the men's room and bought some powder. Giggling, jostling each other and joking loudly they had nearly spilled half of it on the floor as they each took turns snorting up a line of the powder using a rolled up five dollar bill. As Jack recalled, they

hadn't paid $100 per gram for it then. He really liked the high he got. What a rush, such colors and wild amplified sensations. All the girls in the disco suddenly looked really sexy to him and like they all wanted to sleep with him, not that they were just sniffs after a free drink. He had a hard-on for most of the rest of that night and he was sure that every girl in the joint thought he was the sexiest man there. But as high and horny as he was after that first trial with coke, he did not score that night. Maybe the secret was that the girl also had to be snorting the same stuff at the same time, he thought at the time. But he really liked the high. In Murpheysville, coke was not the thing. People there used crystal meth. Although Jack himself hadn't tried it he knew kids at the high school and at the community college he went to who had used it and some had even offered to sell him some. On this night he took the powder back to his rooms and snorted it. Blue and green lights filled the air. Again he felt so strongly aroused that it seemed as if his erection was going to take off and fly around the room. His head spun and all sounds were amplified and there was a loud tinkling of bells, or crashing of breaking glass, or distant whining sirens. His tongue was bitter but also there was a cold sweet sensation on it as if he were chewing on crushed ice popsicles. Manuel had been right; Jack did not see him again. But over Jack's first year in LA he had made contact with this drug distributor 10 times and usually bought coke, when he had spare cash. Transactions were arranged through portable phones

and contacts were always pre-assigned for meetings in cars. On those occasions when he did not have enough for coke, he bought weed and smoked joints. But the euphoria was different. Marijuana was more a relaxant and not a high.

During that same period Jack tried to pick up some girls. On several summer weekends when it was warm enough and when he didn't go shooting or hunting, Jack went down to Venice Beach or Santa Monica and trolled for girls he could pick up. But his come on lines delivered with his distinctly southern accent were completely unsuccessful usually evoking responses like "Drop dead." or a rolling of eyes. He usually would watch the girls in bikinis splashing in the surf or stretched out trying to catch some sun. But approaching the girls he found attractive proved to be near impossible for him. The Chicana girls were not attractive, usually overweight and dark skinned. They always went around in groups and would as a group often laugh and point at him if he approached too closely. Standing at the surf's edge watching the attractive girls in the water, he caught himself doing the same thing as many young Mexican boys in black swim shorts. That first summer he did not yet have many tattoos and so he was not so self-conscious. He couldn't imagine himself like some of the skate boarders on the boardwalk in their surf shorts and brief tops who were covered everywhere with tattoos. He swore that he would never cover himself completely with tattoos. He thought it looked awful--like a circus freak, or a member of biker gang, or a prison inmate, or

a Venice Beach skateboarder. He tried swimming in the surf but found the water was too cold, even though the air was hot on the days he went. On one day he was sitting in the sand about 12 feet from a girl in a red bikini. He found himself staring—nearly in a trance--at the red mound of her left breast, closest to him, and lost track of how long he had been staring at her. A man, who must've been her boyfriend for the day, got up and walked over to Jack. He kicked some sand up at Jack. "Hey you scum bag, beat it. Go someplace else to gawk at the girls." Jack clumsily stumbled up, angry. But he did not challenge the other man, who looked like a California muscle man, broad shouldered, heavily muscled, tanned, and five inches taller than Jack. Abashed, Jack moved on down the beach. It wasn't the first time he had been humiliated by a big boy. Jack wasn't small, he was five foot ten, but thin and wiry. When he was a sophomore in high school and he was trying out for the varsity football team, a big senior named Buddy had given him a big hit when he tried to block him and had crumpled him to the ground. The play was over, but Buddy came back over to Jack, still on the ground and batted his helmet rattling it hard. "Bobby's little brother is a runt. Couldn't knock over a bale of hay." laughed Buddy. Jack, who at that time was even shorter and lighter, was furious and stinging with shame. Later during this scrimmage, he got his back on the sidelines. Buddy was sitting on the bench and as Jack passed behind the bench, helmet in hand, he swung the helmet out as hard as he could, a full hay-

maker, straight into Buddy's face. Buddy's nose exploded with blood and the weight of the blow knocked him backwards off the bench. Jack was ready for Buddy to come after him and thrash him, but instead Buddy was blubbering and crying on the ground, blood spurting over his face and staining the top of his training shirt. Jack was kicked off the football team that same afternoon and he did not try again in later years to join. There on Venice Beach there was no occasion to strike back at the beach boy who had kicked sand at him. On that occasion he went to a bar on the promenade and had a beer. He had had other fights in high school. Once even he had gotten suspended for a week, but he never came out as the winner. Another time he was attacked by an older boy who like the beach boy thought Jack was paying too close attention to his girlfriend. That time the two of them had scrapped and kicked and thrown each other around the central corridor until the school guard came and knocked both of them on the head and stopped the fight. As Jack sat that time at a table on Venice Beach he thought again about his one girlfriend in high school, Annalyn. He did not pick her up, she made a move on him late in their junior year. She was plain looking, pimply faced, with straw colored hair, but she had a very fulsome chest. They had been in English class together after he had already joined the career training auto repair courses in the second half of the day. One day after that class but before he went off to the shop she had approached him and asked him if he would drive her home at the end of school. After that he and

Annalyn hung out together in the school corridors, at lunch hour, --she often hanging on his arm--and then after school they would drive together. But at that time he had already started working afternoons after school at his father's garage. So he usually would drive Annalyn home and then on to the garage. After a few weeks like that Jack and Annalyn started go out driving on Friday or Saturday evenings on a date, sometimes to a restaurant, sometimes to the movies, where he could wrap his arm around her shoulders and dangle his hand down to her right breast. In the movie hall nobody was watching them and he was able to caress her all over. Afterwards they would go driving and park in a shady dark place and spend the evening kissing and caressing each other. They never really talked about anything. And their petting and groping advanced steadily until late in the summer between their junior and senior years, he began undressing Annalyn, going first to take off her top and then fumbling with her bra until it too fell off. She cooperated between kisses. But soon he was kissing her nipples more than her mouth. And what round, glorious white breasts she had. He thought at the time that she could pose for *Playboy* with those big round breasts, not realizing that she was not tall enough to be a *Playboy* model or that her face would need a re-working. Sitting there on the Venice beach promenade coddling a bottle of Dos Equis beer, Jack suddenly realized that out of these pleasurable memories, it was the figure of the naked Annalyn lying on the front seat of his pick-up truck five summers

before which had stuck in his memory and which he saw again on the hood of the Mercedes not long before in the shop. The thought excited him. He knew he had seen that figure before. In those former summer evenings he had had his first sex with Annalyn, most nights in his truck, but also every night in her bedroom when her parents had gone for a week long casino vacation in New Orleans and had left her behind alone in the house. He learned that she normally slept naked. The first time he had penetrated her, she tensed up, and sharply said, "Pull out before you come, Jack." Otherwise she did not seem to enjoy the sex. After ejaculating into a kleenex he wanted to get into her pussy again, but she was reluctant afraid of getting pregnant. But they did have multiple couplings and she did cling to him and hiss out "Love me, Jack, Oh Jack, Love me." throughout the nights when he was in her bed. "Why don't you tell me you love me, Jack?" she whispered as she wrapped her arms around his neck. "I tell you that I love you. But you don't say anything." Another time she had asked him gently, "You know you seem to always look angry? Did you know you grind your teeth?" He didn't know how he looked to others, and Annalyn was the first to tell him. But after having interrupted sex she would go back to the refrain. "Do you love me? Say that you love me, Jack." He never answered her. He wasn't sure he loved her. It didn't seem like love, even though they were having sex. Once he had grunted in reply simply, "uh ghun." And another time, still with a hard erection, he replied by asking her to give him fellatio. "Yeah, suck me.

Suck my dick." Annalyn looked at him suddenly alarmed and pushed a little away from him, "Yew. Yuck. That's sick. Disgusting." He had tried to push his penis to her face but she pushed away even stronger than before, until finally she jumped out of the bed and ran to the bathroom. She wouldn't suck him that evening, nor in any other night after that. It was the incident that pushed them apart. By the start of their senior year they were no longer seeing each other and they looked the other way when they ran into one another in the corridors of the school. All this he remembered late one summer afternoon on the Venice Beach boardwalk. The beach where he couldn't pick up any girl. The only thing he picked up from the Venice Beach boardwalk was an orange death's head skull some Mexican vendor was selling for cheap from a display of dozens of these skulls laid out on the ground.

He also tried to pick up a girl on a Friday night at a night club-disco with similar lack of success. The first time he tried, Jack had chosen a night club that advertised and which sometimes had been mentioned in the entertainment news. It was a long drive up from his apartment, up near Hollywood. And when he finally arrived he found that he was dressed inappropriately, he looked like he was dressed for a hip hop dance club in his jeans, a white tee shirt with the words "Death's Head" printed on it, and a baseball cap. He did not pass face control and was denied entry by the bouncer who

told him “No low lifes admitted. You look like a grease-monkey.” Jack understood that his hands and fingernails gave him away. They were always stained by dirty oil as were his white trainers. The bouncer was black, and although he was dressed in an expensive sharks tooth grey wool suit he looked too big and too mean to Jack to hope he would ever get by him. He hated blacks—always had—and especially he hated black men who held positions of authority or power. He had hated them on his high school football team, because they were so naturally talented, and he hated black policemen he saw in LA. He tried again at a disco club in Inglewood on another night and he successfully got past the black doorman without difficulty. Maybe it was the new black dress shoes he wore. In this club there were lots of black and chicano couples dancing and some Anglos but very few unattached white women. It was a very noisy, busy place with low lights and lots of dancers and many tables. Everyone was dressed in expensive stylish clothes, again not the funk rapper style. He had money in his pocket and he thought he would offer a girl a drink at the bar. He walked up to one shapely woman dressed in a vermillion dress who was leaning heavily against the bar. He stood next to her for some moments, the barmen took no notice him and the woman also ignored him. She was not drinking. She had long black hair hanging down her back and she was looking at a phone. She didn’t act like a sniff. Jack motioned to get a barman’s attention and when he finally caught one before making an order for a drink,

he motioned to the girl, as if to say 'Would you like me to order you a drink?' but before he could say anything to the vermillion woman she turned languidly to him, looking at him disdainfully, and she said, "Don't even think about it, Buster. You can't afford me." And she turned her head away from him again. The barman laughed at Jack and moved to another customer. Later Jack asked a girl who was harboring a drink and standing alone at a drinks table if she would like to dance with him. She at first reacted as if she hadn't heard him. "My name's Jack." He shouted. "If you're free maybe you'll dance with me." The girl reacted then as if she were shy, smiling, waving her hand a little and almost seeming to giggle. She said a few words and it was clear she was Hispanic. Jack stood there opposite her and again she tried to wave him away with her hand, still smiling embarrassedly. She had a super figure sharply outlined in her dress. After looking at each other for several minutes without trying to break through the oppressive noise of the club's amplifiers, two dark haired men in black slacks and pressed white shirts slid through the crowds toward the table, one walking up next to the girl the other stepping up closer to Jack. They looked like gang members. They both glowered at Jack. "You had better leave, Gringo. Go someplace else if you know what's good for you." Jack backed off and walked back around the dance floor and then back to the bar, which ran the length of the back wall. At the other end he could see the vermillion woman still standing against the bar. He

ordered a daiquiri, but was upset when it was brought to him. Fifteen dollars was lot for a small, weak daiquiri with too much ice. He left shortly after concluding that night clubbing was no way to pick up girls.

Not long after that late summer afternoon on Venice Beach, Jack went to Weedhead with the photo he had taken from the bumped up Mercedes and asked if he could put such an image on his chest and torso. Weedhead agreed, but said it would take two sessions at least. "Do you want me to put a name with the figure?" asked Weedhead. Jack immediately thought that putting the name Annalyn would be inappropriate. But there was no other name to put on his tattoo. He simply said no. "Where did you take this picture?" "It was on the hood of a Mercedes." "Oh wow man, that's it. You know that Mercedes is a Spanish girl's name?" "No, no Spanish girl's names." Jack said sternly. "Okay, man, that's cool." It took two long and painful sessions to complete the tattoo. The work was hard and Weedhead fell quiet after working an hour, much to Jack's relief. When Weedhead was finished he stood up. "My masterpiece." he muttered. "Have a look in the mirror." Jack looked and he immediately recognized the image: it was Annalyn lying naked on the front bench of his truck, an imagine just as it had remained lodged in his memory from five years earlier. "What'll ya call your new tattoo, man? Love?" Jack shook his head,no. "Nothing." Weedhead thinks the strangest things, thought Jack as he paid him and left. Almost as if he had read Jack's mind, Weedhead said, "But you know a lot of really weird people come her asking for really

strange things. The other day a real pretty girl wanted me to put a collar tattoo around her neck, with an arrow and the words 'Cut here'. Strange, man. Suicide risk? Go figure." Jack was left with the idea of making love to such a girl and while still coupled cutting her head off along the tattoo with a box cutter. "Yeah, demented, for sure." he muttered as he stepped out the door.

After working most of his first year in LA in Hernandez's garage, Jack changed jobs and became a Mr. Goodwrench in a GM dealership located near Downey. It was an address that was a little farther from his apartment than Hernandez's but the commute to and back was actually faster as it was a dealership located on a freeway. It was entirely more respectable, working hours were shorter although he had to start at 8 in the morning, there was no body work, the usual tasks were mechanical repairs, nearly all the work was for GM cars, Cadillacs and Chevys and the like, so there were few surprises, and most important to Jack there were no illegal Mexican or Salvadorian immigrants working under Panchito's protection. Most of the other mechanics in this shop were Anglos, even a few black men, but as all had to have certification degrees there was a higher level of professional competence in this shop. His work became very routine and Jack appreciated that. The only drawback with this new job was that the pay was less than what Hernandez offered, and taxes were withheld so he had less cash in his

pocket at the end of month and he had to open a bank account so he could deposit and cash his paychecks. But he still did not make any friends with the other staff at the GM garage, preferring to keep to himself. There were no complaints about his work or his punctuality, or his relations with clients, but his manager was concerned that he did not fit into the team at this garage. But he did not disrupt that team either, so his manager overlooked Jack's anti-social behavior. If Jack held racist views about the few black mechanics in the shop, or a low regard for his bosses, he did not enunciate them while he was working there. He never asked for raises or for greater responsibilities. Only once he asked if the Mr. Goodwrench organization would let him take a training course. He gave a hand written note to his boss requesting that he get 'training on Advenced Daignostic Systems' explaining in the note that more and more cars were computerized. He did not get that training. His boss suggested that he go to night classes at a local technical college to get those qualifications. Jack didn't do that. Ironically after his work in a Chicano shop, he was then working in a neighborhood that had a serious problem with Chicano and Salvadorian youth gangs. Many of the cars he worked on over the next two years were cars which had been stolen by gang members and later recovered after having been driven hard for several months and then abandoned. He never thought much about whether he enjoyed his work. He didn't find it challenging and it was just something to do. It seemed to him he had always worked in a garage for his livelihood, and in

some respects he had as he had first started working in his father's garage after school when he was fourteen, already eight years earlier. He still remembered that first when his father picked him after school and took him to his garage. Jack had been so proud then and so grateful for his father's trust and approval. Even though he first worked on simple tasks in his father's garage, oil changes, brake work, tire alignment, he couldn't spend enough time in that first garage. This job in a modern service center was very routine and it gave him a little more time to himself. And soon after he started at the GM garage, he began a very Los Angeles activity-- cruising the streets in his pick-up truck just looking for anything on the streets which might interest him. During the day he worked in almost total isolation and quite, but in the evenings he became a prowler. He did not go cruising every evening. Maybe only once or twice a week for an hour or two. He got to know more about the streets and residential streets of south LA and its many neighboring suburban towns which often blended together. After only a few weeks he discovered a street where after 9 pm the prostitutes paraded their services, sometimes flashing their asses at passing cars. They were Hispanics. There was another street in the far reaches of Inglewood, where the hookers were black girls. Tall and noisy, there was no question about their profession, they advertised and shouted at the passing cars. Finally after several weeks of cruising, he stopped at the curb on the street with Hispanic hookers and opened the passenger

side window. Two hookers came over and looked into the truck at him. One called him Jimmy. She switched immediately into English. “Looking for a good time, Jimmy?” She was plump and short, dressed in white shorts and her tummy stuck out from beneath her half halter type shirt while her breasts nearly hung out of the v-neck on the top. The other was a little taller, who was preening as if she was standing at a mirror. She had dyed her hair a light color but still had mocha colored skin and good teeth, and wore a very skimpy, short blue dress. Jack made a deal with the taller girl and she opened the door and hopped in. After sex, he dropped her back near the street where he had picked her up.

He was maybe five or not quite six years old when he regularly played with his neighborhood buddy Randy. Randy lived in a white clapboard house at the edge of the same neighborhood as Jack’s and had been his playmate since they were very little. They were playing behind Randy’s house in a wooded area that sloped down to a small, sandy bottomed stream that was hidden from sight of the house. A secret place where they often played, hunting for salamanders, or throwing stones at birds or pendulous hanging paper wasp nests, or pretending to be pirates searching for buried treasure. One warm day, Randy’s older sister Cindy, who was maybe nine years old then, but to Jack seemed so old and mature, came down from the house and found them. “Hey guys come here. I’ll show you something you’ll like.” She kneeled down on her knees and they stood in front of her. “We can play adults.” she said. “Here take down your pants.” Randy very promptly

was about 11 or 12 years old he did see Cindy again, a mature looking teenager with a pronounced figure wearing a tight fitting orange dress. She was hanging on the arm of her high school boyfriend, a pimply faced senior with a football varsity jacket and a silly smirk on his face. Jack wondered if she sucked his penis, and if that was the reason for his expression like that of a contented cow. Once at Pacho's he saw a young woman bring in her Cadillac for servicing. She was wearing a bright orange dress, and he was immediately reminded of Cindy, but she had already rushed off by the time he could move to get a closer look. A couple of other times around LA he glimpsed what he thought also looked like Cindy in an orange dress. Maybe she had followed him to LA? Maybe she was spying on him because she still secretly liked him.

At about the same time in his life when he was eleven or twelve, Jack had started looking at the color-printed sex magazines. He had a school friend named Dan who invited him over sometimes to his house after school. It was there in the family room that Jack first saw copies of *Playboy* which Dan's father bought and left stacked on the low table in the TV room. He and Dan looked through them at the naked models, laughing, pointing, and staring at the models' breasts and pussies. Once Dan went into a closet and brought out a couple more hard core pornographic magazines, like *Hustler*, which his father hid in the house because they showed more explicit sex. It was there that he saw pictures of naked women performing fellatio on men with huge penises, and other photos of full penetration sex. Jack liked

these magazines from the start and almost every visit to Dan's house included a perusal of them. And afterwards, back at his own house in the evenings in the bath he began his regular practice of masturbating—although at that time without result-- a practice he followed for the rest of his life. He wondered if Dan's father used those magazines with Dan's mother. He did not long mix with Dan. Dan and his family moved to Nashville only about a year later. Jack did not hear any more from Dan after that. And he did not have any further access to the pornography magazines until after he left the house. He couldn't buy them until he was eighteen and even then his father would never have allowed him to bring them into the house. Once he joined the army, Jack was able to buy *Hustler* and other porn magazines and he had them in Afghanistan, although the army discouraged soldiers from having them in the country. After he moved to LA, Jack was a regular user of the pornographic sites on his computer. The first girl that he had sexual intercourse with was Annalyn of course, but he thought then and afterwards that it was not really love. She was attractive but not really pretty and she never did really turn him on. She did not fit the ideal images of pulchritude that were displayed in the porn magazines. But she did introduce him to sex. And it was Annalyn who also had introduced Jack to crystal meth. She had started using it when she was an early teen having been introduced to the stimulant by her meth-addled older brother. Crystal meth use apparently was widespread in Murpheysville

when Jack was in high school. After they stopped seeing each other in his senior year at high school he stopped using crystal meth completely. It was then too expensive for him and the reactions and after effects were too unpleasant. He also didn't see Annalyn after that for almost three years. After he got back from Afghanistan and returned to Murpheysville briefly he did see Annalyn once, by accident. In the interim, she had gotten married, had a child and she had lost a lot of weight and looked drawn and haggard. He ran into her on the sidewalk in the downtown one bright day, and almost did not recognize her. She looked much deteriorated-- like many of the meth heads—and harassed with a toddler tugging at her arm. He wondered how he ever found her to be sexy or attractive. He did not want to see her again after that last chance encounter.

As a young teen, before Jack had started working at his father's garage, Jack played flag football as an after school activity on the field behind the junior high school. It was a loosely organized program, which was open to 13-14 year olds who attended that school. Usually games drew 20 to 26 boys who would divide up into the two teams and put on their red or yellow flags. It was not the full contact football game: blocking was allowed, but not tackling, and no one wore helmets or pads. There was one adult, a teacher, who provided some refereeing and distributed the equipment which belonged to the school. Jack played alongside his friend Randy. One cool autumn afternoon, they were playing on the same side. Jack

was playing as a fly back, because he ran fast and was good at catching the ball. Randy, who was bigger, was playing as a halfback responsible for some blocking for the quarterback. On one play, a black boy, who was prematurely big and heavily muscled for his age, and known around the school for being rough, ran hard straight into Randy knocking him flat to the ground. The referee whistled play to stop. And what happened next Jack would never forget. He came over as other boys were gathered around Randy, who was convulsing on the ground and making frightening gagging noises. Jack had never seen anything like it before. Randy's eyes were rolled up inside his head so only the whites could be seen, his mouth was frothing, and he jerked violently from left to right, his head jerking spastically. The adult ran over, kneeled down over the boy and then got out his mobile phone and called the ambulance service. In the 15 or so minutes it took an ambulance to arrive, Randy's spasms continued, he began to turn blue in the face. The teacher did not know what to do, but he said it was epilepsy. The black boy was apologizing and crying. "I didn't mean to hurt nobody." Tears stained his dark cheeks, and his mouth was twisted up in grief and pain. The other boys stood around mutely. When the medic came, he took one look at Randy and said, "He's swallowed his tongue. Did anyone try to get it out?" No one had. He worked at retrieving Randy's tongue but by then his teeth were clenched and he worked to no avail. Randy was already dead. The medic carted Randy's stiff body in the ambulance, and

the other boys started to drift away. Jack looked at the black boy, whose name he did not know, and shouted, “You bastard. You killed him.” The others began shouting at him too. The big black boy whined, “No, man, no I didn’t kill nobody.” And he ran away. The black boy did not come back to that school for almost a month. Jack hated him on sight ever afterwards, in the corridors or outside. There were other blacks in the school, not many, but Jack readily transferred his contempt from the one who killed his best friend to all of them and kept that feeling through into high school. Jack attended the funeral for Randy feeling that he could have somehow prevented the accident. It was on a frosty day when the leaves were flying around the cemetery, and the sun setting early provided almost no light or heat. He associated death and misery ever after to such late autumn afternoons.

This time, the cocaine seemed stronger and gave him an immediate rush. The lights swimming around his room in front of his eyes were more intense, sharp purple and blue, and yellow. His breathing was faster and seemed as if iced. His head was throbbing and his penis stood erect like a giant mushroom. He spun around the room as if his feet were six inches off the floor. Somehow he didn’t know how, he ended up in his truck, driving fast to the street with Chicana prostitutes. Next thing he knew he was driving along the freeway eastbound with a plump mocha colored woman with big breasts silently sitting to his side on the bench seat. She said her name was Linda. The road swayed from side to side around the truck, the

oncoming cars and trucks on the other side of the highway all seemed to be flashing their lights in his eyes. The mountain road, however, was dark and he thought there were bats by the thousands flying out of the corners of his eyes, out of the deep gloom of the roadside trees. He stopped the car and pulled off his pants and shirt and Linda began to suck his oversized penis. Warm and pulsating colors were waving through him. Then Annalyn slipped off his chest and tucked her legs under Jack as she reclined invitingly back onto the bench seat of his truck. She was cooing at him and the truck cab seemed as if plunged in a pulsing lavender light—but it was not dark, instead everything became bright as if the sun was shining over his shoulder even though it was the middle of the night. He slipped into her vagina, and she was muttering, "Oh big man. Come inside me. So manly, your member. Fuck me good." But Jack felt nothing. She had a loose vagina. He was humping Annalyn but to no effect, there was no sensation. His hands then wrapped around Annalyn's throat and he began constricting on her neck. Linda tried to gasp and began to struggle and then Annalyn's vagina tightened around his penis and her hips violently convulsed. It was the most extreme pleasure Jack had ever felt, and the rush of his ejaculation came through him like an wide electric stream up from his feet or down his spine and through his lower gut toward to the new center of his existence deep within his penis. He was sweaty and breathing heavily and his head still spinning when this tremendous sensation finally

subsided and the night's darkness returned to the truck's cab. Linda was still and silent as he pulled out of her. He sat up behind the wheel of the truck and dozed off for what seemed like hours. Finally the effects of cocaine and sex wore off and he needed to urinate. When he got back in the truck he searched for his pants and a pack of cigarettes. He smoked slowly. Linda still had not moved. He dressed and then nudged Linda, who did not respond. She was dead. In the next hour nothing was clear in his mind, which was still flustered by the cocaine high. He pulled Linda's body out of the car and carried her –she was not heavy at all-- to the side of a deep gully where he threw the body in. It crashed loudly through the dense underbrush and disappeared. He collected her skimpy clothes and put them in a nylon bag. He looked up in the western sky and saw the pale orangey glow of LA on the clouds. It was like the colors still swirling in his head. Then he backed the truck back onto the road and began the long drive back to LA and to home, stopping at a large trash bin where he tossed out the sack with Linda's clothes. It was the first of several times over the next four years that the tattoo of Annalyn came to life for him. Once several months later Jack looked at himself in a mirror and was surprised to see something he had not ever noticed before about his Annalyn tattoo. There now seemed to be little splotches of red—an ink color that Weedhead had not used on the original tattoo—on the figure's neck, around the corner of her lips and on her crotch.

His work as Mr. Goodwrench continued to be very routine. He usually performed very mundane repairs on motor parts that were worn out. Owners would raise a fuss and direct their anger at him. "Designed obsolescence! These parts always wear out the instant their warranty ends!" But he could handle those clients, largely because he agreed with them. Still he felt that these clients were blaming him for the car's defects, and he resented it. After letting them rant—and so many did all in the same way—nearly always these clients would calm down and authorize him to order the replacement parts and fix the problem. The clients who were more of a problem were the ones who came in complaining of an indistinct squeaking or wheezing sound somewhere in the car more usually in the engine when it was running. These clients were hard to mollify. They expected perfection and demanded that the sounds be eliminated, but in Jack's experience, he could never find these mysterious, obnoxious sounds. Sometimes he would take a drive with the owner and still Jack could not hear these so called defect noises. Sometimes he would hear occasional squeaks in the brakes or springs, and more often, a small squeak in the front dashboard where the sealant between the car's steel body and the plastic dashboard was missing. When he told the owners this was the only problem and likeliest cause of the sound, these owners would fly into rages aimed at him, calling him a country imbecile, an unqualified engineer, a fraud, a lazy sonnofa bitch, or worse. He realized that he was like the doctor who was

abused and forced to give his patients the drugs they wanted or they would make a huge ruckus or sue for incompetence. He invariably submitted to doing some sort of repairs—usually on the brakes or the springs—in an attempt, often times in vain, to mollify the clients and to address the unknown squeak. He thought once it would be funny if he presented a more mild-mannered client with a dead mouse, claiming he found it in the engine, but he thought better of that. Invariably, just like the doctor who gives placebos finds out, the client would be satisfied for a very short while before he discovered that the sound had returned, only louder and more insistent. Then Jack would get upbraided by the boss and chief mechanic in front of the client, and he would be removed from working on that client's car. But in general in the four years he worked with this GM dealership as a genuine Mr. Goodwrench, he felt contented with his work. It was not demanding—other than dealing with obstreperous clients-the hours were not too long, the pay was good –he got regular pay hikes in those years—he did not have to work with a team or with any of the other mechanics, especially not with the two black mechanics whom he found to be noisy and opinionated, and the shop provided him with an overalls uniform so that he did not have to pay anything to clean his clothes. Throughout his years in LA he invariably wore the same clothes, a tee shirt—most often an Atlanta Braves tee shirt— a pair of faded blue jeans, sneakers, and a red baseball cap, also with the red A of the Braves on it. His entire wardrobe had come with him from Tennessee and by his third year at

Mr. Goodwrench it was beginning to wear out and look a little frayed so he needed to replace the tee shirts and jeans, but he didn't know how to find and shop for these items. He told himself he would buy some new clothes at a Walmart's but he either never had the time to spare from his regular activities or he didn't have the money at the moment when he had the spare time. So he was very content that the shop gave him clean work overalls which he would put on every morning. But he was also contented by the pay. By his third year he was earning more than $17 per hour. Of course like everyone in the shop he bitterly resented the taxes that the shop took out of the paycheck, but he still earned enough to cover all his expenses and to support his cocaine habit, his dues and expenses at the shooting club, and his occasional use of prostitutes. During this time he gave up looking to meet up with girls at nightclubs, because it was so expensive and so futile. And he stopped going to the beach in the summer because he had no more success there, and he no longer wanted to take his tee shirt off, which would expose his tattoo of Annalyn reclined after sex. He was a little ashamed of his tattoos and did not want to show them off to anybody, which was why he did not get any "sleeve" tattoos or any on his upper neck or head—something Weedhead was always trying to sell him whenever he went there. Jack did notice that there were several very pretty, well-dressed young women in the front showroom of the dealership in front of the service garages. But it was nearly impossible for him to go

there in his overalls. He looked too much like what he was: a poor redneck grease monkey. The one time he tried to see the girls in the showroom not only did the manager shoo him out, but the girls snubbed him as if he were a piece of dog shit tracking filth across the floor. So he gave up trying to talk them up also and only occasionally saw these girls at a distance as they were coming or leave work. His only contacts with women were the Chicana prostitutes he picked up once or twice a month on the weekend. That cost him $100 a pop, but he got his pressing need for sex fulfilled and was contented for another week or two afterwards. Jack kept with the Hispanic girls of the night even though he often drove by a stretch of streets where black hookers were on parade. He never looked at them, but he could see so many of them had fat, round buttocks and big thighs which were quite saliently displayed and the sight disgusted him. By his fourth year in LA, his dark blue pick-up truck was also getting old and long in mileage. He had bought it already slightly used in his junior year in high school so it was already 9 years old and had more than 100,000 miles on the odometer. He maintained it in good shape but each year this maintenance cost him more and more as he replaced worn out parts. He wanted any replacement to also have the front bench seat, instead of the two independent bucket seats, and these were hard to find in LA—as rare in LA as a pick-up truck with a gun rack in the back window. He would have to special order such a truck and pay more, so this was a purchase he continued to put off. He spent more and more of his

free time thinking about how he was going to find a replacement truck and how he was going to be able to pay for it if he found one. Through the internet he could only find used trucks that fit his desire, some were even older than his. Dealers sold only new trucks and none of them had bench type seats anymore, at least not in LA. One dealer told him he'd have to go to Texas to find those features in a new truck. He needed it badly, because he continued to have sex with prostitutes only on the bench seat in his truck. So he began to work with the goal of buying a new truck, and that meant he needed to save money. Other than buying a truck, he did not really see any objective to his work, and he did not really look forward to any future changes or developments. The job and the work suited him and it filled the time and paid him enough for his small needs. He drew no closer to the other mechanics at the garage and he couldn't say he counted any of them as a friend. Indeed during work hours he scarcely spoke to any of them, except in the simplest of matters of completing his work, "Have you seen my number 7 wrench?" "How can I order a disc brake liner for an old Chevy?" But no conversations. And no one tried to converse with him or strike up any comraderie. His boss knew he was not really a team player, but then he did work well and most of the actual work did not entail more than one mechanic at a time working on a car.

He did continue to buy cocaine and use it on weekends, maybe once or twice a month, often on the nights when

he would go out cruising to pick up a hooker. These nights were becoming one of his biggest expenses. Sometimes these were nights when Annalyn would again slip off his chest and onto the bench seat of his truck and give him a good fuck. The highs and euphoria from the cocaine were however wearing thin, not as intense or thrilling as when he had first got to LA and started buying off the street. He suspected his dealers were cheating him, giving him adulterated product. His dealers, always Mexican but not always the same Mexican, kept changing contact and hand over points, and the price for a small dime bag kept inexorably rising. It seemed to Jack that after three years of using this factory's coke that he was getting unpleasant after effects on the day after. Sometimes they were merely headaches or feelings of heavy lassitude or even feeling depressed, but other times he began seeing disturbing and horrifying hallucinations both during the high and sometimes even on the day after. He never remembered faces of the girls he picked up nor the sex he had with them on the evenings when he got high. But on the day after he often thought he could see them haunting him like ghouls, pointing accusingly at him, uttering something through bloodied lips but without sounds. And he began to feel in the days after taking coke a feeling that people everywhere were pointing at him, staring at him and wishing him ill, or thinking that he was an incompetent and dangerous loner. Sometimes he even had vivid dreams where he would see his father again beating him, shouting at him, and calling him an evil, lazy and vile

creature. He even remembered a long suppressed occasion when his brother Bobby had turned on him and hit him so hard that he broke his cheek. He had adored Bobby and he never understood why he had punched him so viciously on that day more than ten years before. Jack began to think that maybe the Mexicans were selling him impure or adulterated powder deliberately to snuff him out. Finally one evening when he went out to find a nickel or dime bag, he instead asked his vendor if he could sell him crystal meth. He had understood it was a lot cheaper and that it was much higher purity than the old brown "home-brew" meth that he had once used in Murpheysville. The Mexican told him that he would have to "order" it in advance, that someone else dealt in crystal meth. So it was in the next month that he first began to use crystal meth. And what a difference the buzz was, the euphoria was even stronger than he remembered from the first time he had used coke in LA almost four years earlier, the whirling lights around his head, the sexual arousal and long erections, the colors and the intense noises which amplified the background music into a blaring cacophony. Euphoria lasted longer –almost all night and into the next morning. He would wake up late, thirsty and dry, needed to piss, on a Saturday or Sunday and he would not know exactly what had happened in the interval between taking the drug the night before and that afternoon.

This was about the same time that Jack started looking at detailed stories about mass shootings. At first he fell on the site about the Columbine High School shooting in Colorado and he spent all evening reading about it, morbidly examining all the details that could be found and following all the links to other information. The two shooters especially interested him not so much by their motivations but by their amateurish handling of the shooting. It was clear to Jake that they did not know anything about shooting the rifles they had and so they wasted a lot of ammunition with little effect. He also could not understand why they committed suicide, especially, if as it was everywhere written, they were taking revenge on their schoolmates, a motive he could well understand and empathize with. Jake did not buy the explanations that the two shooters were mentally ill. He reasoned that if no one had noticed or diagnosed those supposed mental illnesses and psychological disorders before the shootings, that the diagnoses offered by the investigators' psychologists were just bunk and unfounded conclusions of people who needed to justify their own positions and to dismiss the real reasons for the murders. After spending a couple nights studying the Columbine shooting, Jack began to read up on the Virginia Tech shooting which had occurred in 2007, while he was in Afghanistan. He had not heard of it at the time because of his absence, but he was interested because the shooter seemed to be such a fanatic. He was very inclined to think that the shooter, a young Korean-American student, was insane, because after all he reasoned aren't all Koreans crazy and prone

to running amok. In Afghanistan he had seen several young Korean Americans run amok, so to speak lost all self-control and fear, slobbering at the mouth and screaming while running perilously around the base camp. One even had to be shot to be subdued. Jack assumed that all Koreans were like that. And so he looked at the stories on the web about the mad Cho who ran around the VTech campus with no other motivation other than the need to shoot people. Jack was fascinated by the stories and the details about how Cho shot people. He was interested also that Cho seemed to be a better gun handler than the high schoolers at Columbine.

Eventually Jack came upon the references to the Norway massacres of Anders Breivik which had happened only a year before. It had received only cursory coverage in Los Angeles so he learned about the outline of Breivik's killings for the first time through the internet stories and analyses. What really attracted him was that Breivik seemed to have had a manifesto and program which justified and indeed mandated the shootings of 70 or so young people. And unlike a lot of shooters Breivik seemed to know what he was doing. He even escaped alive and did not commit suicide. Jack studied this incident for nearly a week. After work, he rushed home eagerly to continue delving into the story which became more and more attractive as he learned more. He looked up the political program which Breivik had composed as

justification for his shootings of privileged liberal white kids. But apparently it had been deleted from most websites. He found a translated copy, which websites everywhere had claimed had been suppressed, and began to read it slowly and carefully. He found himself intrigued and often agreeing with Breivik's assertions.

About the same time one evening Jack got a call on his cell phone. Caller ID did not work, so he answered it cautiously. "Hello, Jack? Is that you? This is Jose Menendez. Remember me?" In fact it was the first time in almost four years that Jack had heard from Jose. "Yes, Jose, I remember. Is that you? Still here in Los Angeles?" "Yes, yes, and you? Are you still here?" "Sure. Long time, no see. Are you still in cartooning?" "Yes, it has been a long time, but I'm still at it. But I'm calling because it has been such a long time since we met. Jack, I wanted to tell you about an upcoming meeting of a local group of Afghan war veterans. And I thought to invite you. Maybe we could meet again at this meeting." Jack's immediate reaction was reluctance. He never could see the sense in reunions, especially when the meetings were with strangers that he had never met or known. Most of the conversation that followed was dominated by Jose's efforts to persuade Jack to come. Apparently Jose had been to several of these veterans affairs and although he too had been a loner and outsider while serving in Afghanistan, he had met some people he liked. "It would be a barbecue, there'll be beer and it's really informal. People swap stories about their experiences or their units, and even more useful they tell stories about their

experiences since getting back. You know, things like dealing with the VA hospital, or getting special veterans grants or subsidies. And you know, it will be held in the American Legion Hall down by your way in South Los Angeles." Jose hadn't even asked Jack what he was doing or if he was still working at Panchito's garage. Jack made no pledges, but he took the address and the date and time of the meeting which was going to be the next Friday evening. "We'll see, Jose. Maybe I'll come if I have nothing else important to do." he said as non-committedly as he could manage. Eventually Jose gave up and said goodbye, sincerely saying that he hoped he would see Jack in eight days time. Jack had been on the phone for nearly 24 minutes. His cell phone showed him that that was the longest telephone conversation he had had since he had moved out to LA, nearly four years earlier. Of course, he did not have anything important to do on that next Friday evening, and Jack's curiosity grew throughout the week. He even looked up the meeting hall on his google map program, which estimated it was located a 50 minute drive away from his work at the dealership. On the appointed day, Jack did not decide to go, but after work he found himself driving in the direction of the meeting hall. When he parked nearby, he could see there were about a dozen and a half cars and pick-ups parked around, and yet he still could not decide whether to go in or not. Finally he got out of his truck and slowly approached the American Legion hall. As he got close, he was greeted by a smiling, happy voice of a short

woman dressed in a skirt and wearing her summer camouflage service shirt. "Hi, my name is Shirley. I served in Afghanistan in 2010. Lance corporal in the 10th infantry based out of Kandahar. Come on in, stranger. What is your name?" she said while trying to reach for his hand to shake. He offered it limply, his eyes searching around. "I'm Jack. Jack McGee. I'm from Tennessee." He was embarrassed. "Well, that's swell. I was from Texas, but I'm an Air Force brat, lived everywhere around the US, so I don't really come from Texas, and now I live in LA. They're asking us to register over there. So grab yourself a brew and I'll talk to you later." Jack was a little surprised that the first veteran he met was a woman. He hadn't expected any. In Afghanistan, he knew there were women serving but he never saw any, except for those serving in the nurses corp in the hospital where he recovered from his shoulder wound. At the registration, there were two men who looked older than Jack sitting at a folding table dressed in civilian outfits looking a bit like Jack in jeans, tee shirts and canvas shoes. They had short haircuts and introduced themselves with their names, ranks, and years they served in Afghanistan. They were as chipper and friendly as Shirley. "What'll ya drink, Jack?" And just as Jack was about to take his first sip from a cold bottle, his eyes spotted a plump short man with bare muscled arms and curly black hair whom he thought must be Jose. He was pretty sure that he recognized his face and when the man turned Jack's way, it was clear that he recognized Jack. Jose broke off from the man he was talking to and came over to

Jack, a big smile on his face as if he was greeting a long missing best friend. "Jack, I'm so glad you could come. It's been a long time." Jose pumped Jack's hand for longer than a usual handshake. "I think you'll like the meeting, and you'll find some people here who you could like. What did you think of our greeter, Lance Corporal Shirley Blackmon?" Doesn't she look great?" Actually Jack had thought she had looked rather plain—her field camouflage shirt was supposed to make its wearers look plain, if not unnoticeable. And he thought she looked ridiculous in that shirt with a short black skirt which emphasized her heavy legs. "Sure, sure." said Jack, just as Shirley excused herself and went back to the front of the hall. "So are you doing well? You can tell I'm doing all right. I've put on so much weight and now I am a senior animator for a big web game designer. Lots of work, doing more than I ever thought possible. And the pay is real good. Not married yet. Too busy to find a woman." Jack was amazed at the transformation in Jose from the reclusive and taciturn skinny soldier he had first met six years earlier near Kabul, and the voluble, chatty, and decidedly plump Jose in front of him. "Oh, more of the same. I still work in a garage. Keeping busy. I'm also not married." Jack paused a long time. "I think it's hard to meet women here in this city. It's probably easier for you since you came from LA." "Oh yeah, but there are almost no women working at my shop. And I don't socialize much. Spend all my time behind a computer screen, doing computer drawings. Look, I

wanted to introduce you to some of the vets who should come today. We've been having these meetings about twice a year over the past three years." Jose then led Jack back over to the table laid out with salads and appetizers, picked up two, and took a bottle of beer before taking him over to a tall man with a shaved head and dark eyelashes. This was Ace Larner and it appeared he was the oldest person at the gathering. He had been in the Air Force in the early days of the Afghan invasion and after retiring from the Air Force he had become a pilot for a courier air freight company. He looked to Jack like he was in his late forties, but he wasn't. Ace showed no interest in Jack and after some preliminary introductory statements, he excused himself and walked over to Shirley. Jack noticed that the group included only a few black men, but of the rest, the group appeared to be equally divided between chicanos and white men. There was only one other woman in the group, but she clung desperately to a blond man throughout the meeting so he assumed she was his wife. Jose then introduced Jack to another tall burly white man, with a heavy tan, who looked Jack's age but unlike Jack was smartly dressed in a stiff pressed long sleeve white shirt and khaki dockers. He glowered at all around him as if with profound hatred and did not smile when Jose introduced him. His handshake was painfully strong but thankfully brief, given as if a challenge or test of Jack's manliness. "You know, Conrad, Jack here served in my unit. He was sharpshooter first class. I think he was the best shot in the army in my time in Afghanistan. Better even than

the snipers. He knocked off a bunch of mop heads in a number of fire fights." Conrad's expression softened a bit. "Oh yeah? Where'd you learn to shoot, Jack?" "In Tennesee. My father first took me hunting when I was eight. And we'd go to the target range almost every week after church." "Yeah. I'm from Texas. All the grunts in my units were wimps and whiners. Couldn't shoot the side of a barn at twenty feet. What do you do now?" "I fix cars, sometimes do body work. I'm a mechanic. Work in a garage in Downey." "Did you sign up for the National Guard after you left service?" "No." "That's a shame. You should. I was in the marines and when I left I joined the Guard. It was as a guardsman that I was called up for a tour in Afghanistan. It helps keep your martial skills up to snuff. Your shooting skills, for one." "I still practice shooting all the time." "Oh yeah? At a shooting range?" "Yes sir. And I still hunt, although it's not the same as back home." Jack had fallen into his youthful way of speaking to adults and superiors when he said yes sir. "Yeah, I can understand that." said Conrad. "I'm a policeman in the LAPD. Don't get any chance to go hunting, but when I go back home on vacation, I do hunt from time to time." Jack was feeling attracted to Conrad. He reminded him in his forceful confident manner of his brother Bobby. But their introductory conversation was interrupted by the dinner call-- the barbecued ribs were ready-- and if people could get their food, then the program portion of the evening could begin. Jack was very hungry, as he had not had

anything to eat since the early morning and he took a double portion of the ribs and potato salad. He quickly demolished his food washed down by a beer. Before he was finished eating, an organizer got up on a small platform and began to speak. First he gave a brief report on the level of US military involvement still active in Afghanistan, and outlined the president's plan for withdrawal. Then he invited a man to speak about his experiences in Afghanistan. What this man, an Army sergeant, had to say impressed Jack because it was clear that the man had not experienced any fighting during the entire period of his tour of duty. All he could talk about were the American amenities that kept arriving at his camp, the videos, the internet phone connections, the improving food service. It seemed this veteran had hardly any contact with Afghans of any kind, not even translators. Although he did say that his unit did sustain some injuries from roadside improvised bombs. No one wanted to ask him questions. The program ended with a short report about the availability of VA medical services in the LA area. The speaker admitted that there were some delays in getting treatment. Then he added a list of symptoms that could indicate post traumatic stress syndrome. He then called on the veterans sitting around finishing their plates if any of them had good or bad experiences in dealing with the VA. Only one veteran volunteered to give his experience with getting therapy and the difficulties he had in getting a comfortable prosthetic leg. And with that the program was over. Jack went for some more food and another beer, and other people began to go

back to groups of people they knew. Jose came back to Jack who was sitting sucking on some rib bones, and while still standing addressed him: “You know Jack, you should keep in touch. Maybe we could get together before the next one of these veterans meetings. There’s another guy here that I want to introduce you to. Finish up so we can catch him before he leaves.” Jack wiped his fingers on his jeans, stood up and followed Jose across the room to a blond man who was talking animatedly to a small group. Jack could make out a few themes before Jose broke in. “they took us for suckers. The elites support themselves by fostering wars, and killing young men and boys for causes that in no way serve American interests. You know we killed more than a million Afghans, and there’s still no solution in sight over there to their problems. And for this 8,000 Americans were killed. The Twin Tower terrorists were Saudi—not an Afghan among them, but we didn’t make war on Saudi Arabia.” Jose cut in and introduced Jack to the blond man, who was named Marty Bryant. He had been a special ops commando in two tours in Afghanistan. He described how he had started out as a patriot but had learned in five years in Afghanistan that it was all for nothing. Unlike the sergeant who had whined about creatures comforts, Marty had seen lots of heavy fighting. “Jose tells me you were a top sharpshooter, Jack.” “Yeah, you could say that. I like hitting the target every time.” “Were you in a lot of fire fights?” “I don’t know, if you could say a lot compared to your experience.” “Were you

wounded in battle there?" "Well I was shot, here in this shoulder, but I wouldn't say it was in battle. More like in ambulance response service, running out to the site of a IED. Never saw the enemy. They gave me a Purple Heart." "The Afghans were not—and are not our enemies. They are poor victims too. Just poor people scraping out subsistence from the dust." Jack demurred. "I don't know. I rather liked shooting them, whenever I could see them. Shifty bastards." Marty glowered a moment at Jack. "You're sick, man." "They were our enemies. Every one of them. They would slit your throat if your back was turned on them. Better kill them there than let them come here and murder us." "Can't talk to such people." muttered Marty as he turned away from Jack and the others listening to him. Jack went back to the drinks bucket and got another bottle of beer, looking for Jose. Before he could finish his beer, Conrad tapped him on the shoulder. "I wanted to give you this before I left." Conrad offered him a business card, which was printed in color with an American flag and an eagle. "Got to go now. Look them up on the internet address there." The card was printed in bold letters, American National Salvation Militia, and in sub-font it read, Confronting the Menace. Conrad left and Jack decided it was time for him to leave as well. As he was leaving he saw Jose was chatting up Shirley, both laughing and leaning into each other. He didn't say good bye to anyone. As he drove off in his truck, he had a vision of one of his victims. One of the few times when his unit had gone to see who they had shot. He had run ahead and had

been the first to reach the dirt wall where return fire had come from. There were two black clad bundles curled up in the dust, obviously dead, and a third man actually a youngster, was sitting back against the wall, blood oozing from upper chest, his eyes open and tearing, his kalashnikov covered in dust some feet away. It was obvious this Afghan was only a boy, maybe fifteen, maybe less. His eyes looked imploringly up at Jack with a confused pained expression. Jack looked at the other two dead men covered in dust, who still held their guns. He turned to the youngster and shot him dead, only a few seconds before his mates rounded the corner of the wall and reached him. When they questioned him, Jack said simply. "He was going to shoot me." No one made an issue of it, then or later.

His father woke him early that summer morning. He was only fourteen. Bobby was already eating breakfast when Jack came to the table. Their mother was not up yet. The three of them climbed into father's big Dodge Ram truck and drove off by seven. They drove a couple hours to Lafette, just outside the Moorestown Air Force Base. They arrived at the fairgrounds just as a large crowd of men were stepping out of their cars and trucks. Like a tide, they rose up and collected around a podium that had been erected in front of a tent. After some agitated waiting a man climbed onto the podium, tested the microphone, and then began to introduce the special speaker of the day, Duke Dennison, the former grand marshal of the Louisiana

KKK. A young looking blond man with a beaming smile bounded up the stairs to the podium and began a speech with introductions, expressions of thanks for his invitation, his pleasure in being back in Tennessee, and his happiness at seeing some of his brothers in the crowd. Then after finishing a lot of these preliminaries which reminded Jack of his preacher at their church, his face turned more somber and he began to look pained. "My friends, white American society is facing a menacing threat from two groups in this country, and we have to brace ourselves and fortify our efforts to thwart them. You know what people I am talking about. The niggers, and the Jews. They have completely taken over the Democratic Party and that means they run Washington. And they are doing everything in their power to wrest power from white Americans, the people who built this country, the people who gave this country civilization and wealth, the people who make this country great, people like you and me." Jack thought that this Duke Dennison sounded ever more like his preacher. Sometimes it was a little difficult for Jack to understand the speaker's flowery words but his elocution was passionate and full of wind and passionate contempt for his subject. But there were some sentences that stuck to his mind. "Brothers, I tell you the true when I say to you, 'I hate niggers, black folk, or whatever you want to call them'" They call each other mothafuckas, and that is precisely what they are. Sexually deviant beasts who would whip out their male members in a moment to rape and seduce our women. I hate them and everything they stand for.

They are a stain and threat on our good society." Dennison then went into a long diatribe about the evils of the black race, talking about the KKK's long and noble cause to eradicate them, or punish them and push them back to the position where they belonged. Then he turned to the Jews. "And I have to tell you, brothers, that the only people that I hate less than the niggers, are the Jews, the Yids, the masters of New York and world finance, who everywhere enslave us and defile us through their control of money." It was a long speech, after spending ten minutes describing the evils of blacks, he spent the same about of time and same vituperation and venom describing how the Jews, who were not a white race at all, spent all their efforts gouging the last dime out of honest white folk. How they were vampires and greedy money-idolaters, who threatened the true Christian faith as well as white society. And after half an hour in the noontime sun, the speaker finally introduced the American White Nationalist Society, a white supremacist collective that was spreading its word and beliefs all over American. He called for good white folk everywhere to listen to their themes, and to struggle to thwart (he used this word a lot, which was not entirely clear in its meaning to the young Jack) these dual menaces. Finally he got around to what he wanted the crowds assembled that day to do. Of course he wanted people there to subscribe to the American White Nationalist party, but he said "Even if you cannot join our party, I want to tell there are things we should do. And these are what

should we do: We should fight the niggers and Jews at every juncture where we can, and that includes violence, because violence is the only means that will ultimately defeat these kinds of lower people. We should be politically active, and vote the blacks and Jews out of legislatures, out of Washington, and especially out of government. That means we should do everything to deflect the electoral subsidies these peoples get from the courts. That means we should fight against the Democratic Party, which is run for the benefit of Jews, and blacks, socialists, peasant immigrants, and welfare mommas. Bar them from the polls, shut down their offices, harass their candidates, whenever we can. And then we should boycott them in our everyday lives. Don't give them services, don't hire blacks or Jews, don't give your business to their companies, boycott the banks where they work, don't use Jewish lawyers or doctors." Jack thought at the time that he didn't know any businesses in his small town that were owned or run by Jews or blacks. He couldn't even think of any Jews he had ever been aware of in his town or school. The speech droned on, and Jack found it more and more difficult to follow. Only the tone of hatred and the angry vituperation remained with him. Still he heard some little snatches which were direct and clear. "Kill the beasts." or "Burn their churches and synagogues." From time to time the attending audience cheered, but not as Jack remembered at these specific incitements to extreme violence. On the drive home, Jack asked if his father knew of any Jews in Murpheysville. "I think I may

have met one. Ugly shyster, here peddling something or other, insurance I think. But he left. He was from New York. Spoke a real ugly accent." Bobby also had not met a Jew in his years at school. "But there are too many blacks in our school. Shuffling down the corridors like bums with their over-sized jeans and their ass-cracks exposed."

Not even three months after this tent meeting with the former KKK man with a broad smile and a message of hate, in the new school year, Jack was suspended from school for two weeks for beating up a black boy in the hall way between classes. Jack had come upon an argument between the youth and a white girl and two younger white boys. The black boy, whose name Jack did not know, but whom he had seen around the school for some time because he was tall and gangly and looked older than his 16 years, reminded him of Dennis the black boy whose hard block had sent Randy into his fatal epileptic attack. Dennis had since left the school. But still when Jack came upon this argument with the tall black youth shouting at the other three, Jack saw red and he rushed in with his fists flying and pounding on the astonished black youth. Jack's attack was so sudden and forceful that he knocked the taller one to the ground. Jack jumped on him and began pounding him on the head and face. He didn't see a black boy at all. All he could see was Randy's spasms on the ground. He was still beating him, crying and shouting insults, when a school monitor pulled him off the poor victim

who was badly mauled. The school authorities had no choice but to suspend Jack. But his father was not disapproving or angry with Jack. In fact it was during this suspension that his father had taken him on work at his service station, starting his career as a mechanic. He was much more upset when Jack got kicked off the football team later than fall also for fighting.

A few evenings after the veterans' get-together, Jack looked up the website on the card that Conrad had given him. It was the site of a white supremacist group in the LA area. It claimed to be a national party representing white nationalists all across America. It had lots of photos of big highly muscled white guys sporting western hats and mustaches displaying big hunting rifles or semi-automatic rifles. There were articles about the coming apocalypse and survivalism. There was a link to their statement of beliefs. Others were news items about confrontations around the US, statesments made by party leaders, and articles about political enemies of the group both in Washington and locally. There was a lot of criticism of US government agencies that violated Second Amendment rights of members and there were announcements of meetings and upcoming events for local members. As well as announcements of shooting contests to be held at local ranges. A lot of the website, Jack found boring and confusing. But he was energized by the range shooting activities and resolved to go to his shooting club that next Sunday. But one link attracted his attention because it offered articles which were supportive of the Norway massacre by Anders Breivik. Most interesting

to Jack was that through these links Jack found a translated summary copy of Breivik's political manifesto which supposedly had been suppressed. He downloaded it and spent the next few weeks slowly and carefully reading and studying it. He found himself intrigued, even though it was difficult going for him, and he often found himself agreeing with Breivik's assertions.

It was a very different autumn evening ten years after his visit to the tent meeting to hear Duke Dennison, when Jack went back to Weedhead's place for a new tattoo. He didn't have anything specifically in mind but he wanted something that would show Jack as a shooter, a sharpshooter. As he drove over he was trying to visualize an image of a righteous, almost Biblical, avenger shooting the ravening masses who were desecrating all that was sacred. But he could not quite visualize anything. It didn't matter. When he got to Weedhead's salon, he found that the master was busy and all three other stalls were also occupied with tattoo artists applying their inks and needles to bared skin. Weedhead broke away from his client, who was quietly moaning from the pain of the pin pricks, to tell Jack. "Hey, sorry mate. It's been a long time since you last came. Business has really picked up. We're fully booked up all this evening and for the rest of the week too. You should call me and make a reservation. Call in the late mornings, I'm usually not so busy then. Gotta take care of this one now. Call me." Jack left,

feeling really annoyed. On his drive back home as it started to get dark, he could not think of any images. All he could think of was his mounting rage aimed at Weedhead. When he got near his usual pick-up area, he waited by the side of the road, and when the Mexicanos drove by he bought a dime bag of coke. The rest of the evening passed in intense purples, refracted light panels, feelings of rage overflowing through visions of large explosions, volcanoes, jumping up and down on someone's head, a pleasant release of huge anger wrapped in bright and warm colors.

The deputy sheriff for investigations in the western district of Riverside County, Detective Allen Jamieson, was filling in routine paper reports on a hot, dry mid morning one Saturday in late September when he got a call on the land line from one of the patrolmen, a man he did not know personally. "Captain Jamieson, I'm Morton Walleau. We are here up in the scrub hills above Corona and near Lake Mathews, off of Scrub Oak Road. We've found the body of a woman down in a deep gulley." "Yeah, murdered?" "It looks like murder. I understood that you're leading the investigations into the women's bodies that have been found in the county in the past several years." "Yeah, I am." "Well, you'll be interested in this one sir. She's fresh body, probably deposited last night. The insects haven't even started eating her and she's just beginning to bloat." Jamieson was interested. All the other bodies had been either skeletons or so far decayed that very little information could be collected to identify the remains. "Are the forensics team there yet?" "I called

them, they should get here in an hour or two." "Can you tell what race, what age this woman is?" "Well, sir, she was dumped absolutely buck naked. If I had to guess, I would say she is Latina, in her twenties. She clearly has dyed hair. Her neck looks pretty scarred, blue and purple like." "Don't touch anything, Morton, until the forensics crew get there. Call a body removal unit. I'll come over there as soon as I can. We need to get the body into the morgue and examined by the pathologist as soon as possible. Maybe we can get some useful DNA materials off it. How did you find the body, Morton?" "We followed the circling vultures. They had not started feasting though. Even the maggots haven't eaten her." "Great. Try and keep the flies away from her." Jamieson hung up the receiver. He turned to his computer screen and looked up the list of reported missing women from Los Angeles County. Nearly all of them were prostitutes. It was a long list. Some of the women had photos, most did not. But more than half of them were African-American women, black prostitutes, most from the same part of south Los Angeles county. The list included women going back almost thirty years. He felt content that in this case, he did not need to worry about the black women or those who disappeared in the 80s or 90s. At the gulley side, Jamieson surveyed the brushy area and scrub forest surrounding the area. The forensics agents had only just started their work and had not yet put the body in a bag. He could see that any footprints or tire marks from the night before were undoubtedly obliterated by all the

traffic of sheriff's patrol cars, officers, and forensic and recovery agents. He asked if a search had found any clothes or shoes. None had been found. He asked if a photo of the woman's face had been taken. It had. One of the forensics examiners showed him the digital photos. "Looks like there are one or two there that are good enough to be used for identification appeals. We need to get that out by end of day. Make sure Los Angeles county missing persons gets copies. Start the process of posting the printed photos in Riverside, and San Bernardino too. This is all real fresh, people might recognize her straight away." As he was leaving he saw there was a drag trail, where the body had likely been dragged to the top of the gulley. It came from a different direction than that taken by his officers. He walked after the drag trail in the dirt and brush. And then he saw them. First in the drag trail there were three or more footprints where the person carrying the body had walked back from the gulley in the cleared dirt. And then there were tire tracks. He called his inspectors over to look at them and record them. Photos were taken, measurements. It seemed probable that the footprints belonged to a man. And further it was clear that there were both advancing and backing tracks onto a dirt track that went straight onto Scrub Oak Road, some clear enough to see the treads.

Late the next day, he got a phone call from the pathologist at the morgue. "Captain Jamieson, I've got some good news for you about the body that was brought in yesterday. We've recovered semen from it, as well as the girl's DNA. It is clear that she was killed

within eight hours from when she was found. And she died from strangulation, fairly quickly I would say. A man with really strong hands. There were nail marks in the bruised skin. I would also say in the snap results, that she is definitely Latina. Just a guess from her facial features that she is from southern Mexico or Central America, but I am not a specialist in ethno-identification." Jamieson thanked the man and whooped up at his desk. This was a major breakthrough. He looked at his list of missing women who were identified as Latina from Los Angeles, San Bernardino, and Riverside counties. Now with the latest report from the pathologist, Jamieson could only think one thing: 'We have a serial killer on our hands, dumping Hispanic prostitutes here in Riverside County.' The three earlier bodies that had been found over the previous three and a half years had been identified from their bone structure as being probably young women from Central America or Mexico, Latinas. But not one of these bodies had as yet been identified. Now perhaps they had the chance to identify this victim. But he recognized it was still a long shot. Almost never was there a relative or friend who came forward to identify murder victims of these women. Although he had a long list of missing persons from his county and from the neighboring counties, most of them were of women who had disappeared more than ten years ago. He had had long talks with his counterpart in the LA County sheriff's office. Linking a murder victim to the missing persons' list was a rare

event, and identifications were hard to come by. The LA office had told him that they were looking at a probable serial killer, who had been raping and killing prostitutes over the previous eighteen years. His methods were the same: after killing his victims he dumped their bodies in commercial trash dumpsters in poorer parts of the city, usually at night. But in this case, all of the bodies were quickly discovered, usually dressed, and all of them were black women. Still no one came forward from the prostitutes' community to give any evidence about a man picking up women who subsequently disappeared. This looked like four women killed and dumped without clothes, all Hispanics and young, that is, likely prostitutes. Yet the same silence seemed to apply to that group of 'working girls'. Social workers in LA and in LA county where most of the Hispanic prostitutes worked did not get any leads, or even any indication of disappearances, since apparently quite often some girls were abducted and taken back south of the border and disposed of and most of the working girls lived in fear of their pimps.

A few days later, Jamieson confirmed the findings of the pathologist. He had extracted male DNA from the semen that had been recovered. And in the victim's neck he had found evidence that the strangler had traces of some sort of petroleum products under his nails which he had left in the victim's skin as he strangled her. The other inspectors confirmed that from the footprints, the murderer had a size 10 ½ shoe size, and was probably a good sized, strong man. But the prints were of Converse sneakers and that information would

lead nowhere. Everyone in LA seemed to wear Converse sneakers. The same for the tire tracks. They indicated a common brand of tire that was probably on a pick-up truck or a four by four vehicle. Again that was not much help for Jamieson. Another week went by, and then Jamieson got another phone call from patrolman Walleau. "Captain Jamieson, sir, this is Morton Walleau. You know, it was I who called you about four weeks ago when I found the body up on Scrub Oak Road. I was talking with another patrolman, one who has worked the evening patrols up on the mountain roads over the past year and he told me a story that I figured would interest you. He told me that one night four months ago after eleven o'clock, as he was patrolling up in the hills off of interstate, he came up on a naked woman walking on the side of the road. And she hailed him down. She was buck naked except for some shoes, there in the middle of the night on a seldom used mountain road, and she hailed down his car. She could not have known he was a policeman. But when he stopped, and she saw who he was she did not run. She was spouting all kinds of angry banter in Spanish mixed with English. Madder than a wet cat with a rat trap on its tail. She was furious. So this guy, Officer Smithson, offered her a blanket and a ride somewhere. She said a white guy had picked her up in south LA and drove her out here. She even admitted it was for sex. But best he could understand, after they stopped and she had undressed, just as he was getting ready for sex, he stopped suddenly. He asked her what

kind of perfume she was wearing, and when she told him it was lavender, he threw open the door and pushed her out of the damn truck—it was a big old pickup truck with a big front bench seat—and threw only her shoes at her before driving off, leaving her alone and naked on this dark back road. She had already walked she thought about almost two hours, but she did not know where she was. My mate told me that she said it was a dark green or dark blue, pickup truck with out of state plates. So he drove her all the way to East Los Angeles-- can you imagine?--and dropped her off at a house that she pointed out. A funny story, don't you think? But I got to thinking that maybe the guy who picked up this Salvadoran girl, could be the same who is dumping bodies in those hills. He drove a pickup maybe just like the one we detected at last month's murder site. What do you think?" Jamieson was amused. There wasn't much in that story that helped his investigation. No real crime had been committed. He thanked Officer Walleau and hung up.

Jamieson asked the criminal investigation bureau if they had any records of criminals, perhaps sex offenders, those who had served time in prison, whose DNA matched the one that the pathologist had recovered. He didn't get any positive response from the California bureau, but they suggested that he inquire from the Defense Department's veterans records office. It seemed they kept a DNA database of the soldiers who recently had served in the wars in Iraq and Afghanistan primarily as a means of identifying bodies left on the field of battle or blown up by roadside bombs.

Jamieson decided to write to them requesting information if they had any DNA records that matched what they had and which could identify their murderer. After a few weeks he got an official Defense Department letter back from this office, saying that their office kept the DNA records solely for purposes of battlefield identification and not for use in assisting criminal investigations. Jamieson protested to the county prosecutor and requested that the prosecutor's office should make an official appeal to see if they could not get some a matching record that could help identify their serial killer. The prosecutor agreed to file a court request. Jamieson was discouraged. This would take a lot of time. But in months while this request was dragging through the courts, about two months later, the bones of another woman, probably a Latina from the size and form, were found again in the forests of the county's mountains. This time the remains were much older, maybe five or six years old, and there was not much new information that they extracted from them, except that like the others there were no signs of clothes or shoes found with the bones, and an interesting detail showed that the hair had been dyed. When he saw this, Jamieson asked the forensic investigator if the other three bodies had also had dyed hair. The answer came back positive; two of the women had bleached their hair a lighter color than their natural color. To Jamieson this suggested that all of his victims were undoubtedly prostitutes. He then made the connection with the young woman in Walleau's

story and he decided to ask the missing persons bureau of Los Angeles county sheriff's department if they had records or reports of missing Latina prostitutes from the past six years from the area of East Los Angeles where one of his patrolmen had dropped off the Latina Lady Godiva several months earlier. His request drew some interesting information. First the analyst at the LA office told him that someone had come forward to identify the photo of the recently murdered young woman. The informant gave them a name, and approximate place of residence and confirmed that she had worked as a prostitute and had gone missing from her usual display and solicitation locations several months ago. The same analyst told him that their records indicated that there were seven girls who had been reported missing from this part of time over the past six years, all of them the age of prostitutes, 18 to 34 years old. Jamieson put the receiver back down and started to write down a picture of his serial killer. He was looking for a young man with strong hands or arms and large feet who prowls for prostitutes in a large dark green or dark blue pickup truck or four by four vehicle having a front bench seat, possibly with out of state license plates. This man regularly solicits Latina prostitutes in East or South Los Angeles and he drives them out to the mountains of western Riverside County, maybe to remote mountains of the neighboring counties where he murders them after sex an dumps their naked bodies. He has done this four times, possibly more often. He sent this profile to the LA police, the LA sheriff's department, to the San Bernardino city police

and to the San Bernardino county sheriff, as well as to the Orange county sheriff's department.

Jack began to marvel at Breivik's shooting attack in Norway. He was especially impressed by the ideology which Breivik espoused which justified, indeed required such an attack, and he was equally impressed by the planning and the gun handling skills of the calculating killer. He conflated these impressions with the materials and ideology he was reading from the White National party. As these ideas brewed in his head, he came ever closer to concluding that he would have to do the same thing as Anders Breivik; that Jack had to emulate his nationalist hero. He would have to get a rapid fire, semi-automatic rifle and stock up on ammunition for it. In late summer on a Sunday afternoon he went out to his shooting club. He was looking for Kyle, but Kyle was not around that day. Jack did some target shooting on the open range where there were plywood painted targets of elk and buck deer standing at intervals of 200 to 600 yards out across the range. After spending an hour shooting there, he went to the indoor target range where the shooting was from the prone position for the rifle, or kneeling for pistol shooting. Kyle still had not shown up. It had been a long time since he had seen Kyle at the club. Maybe he was no longer a member. Jack did not have his cell phone number so he could not call him. He decided to leave, when he noticed on the public announcements board just what he was going to ask Kyle for. Hanging

on the board, in hand written blue ink, there was a small scrap of paper: For Sale: M4gery Good condition. Reasonable price. Call to arrange details. (909) . . . - . . . . Jack copied the number into his cell phone and planned to call it later. He had to be careful, because he knew, as the seller did, that this would not be a legally registered sale, it was not even going to be a straw purchase. It was a war weapon which we was going to buy on the black market. It was a gun he particularly liked as he had used a very similar type of rifle in Afghanistan. It was not generally available to the civilian gun-buying public.

The more he studied the writings of Breivik, and examined the histories of mass shootings in the US, and other postings on the American White Nationalist party website, the more Jack began thinking of doing a mass shooting, of going after the people who persecuted him and made him feel inferior. He began to think he could do better than many of the other shooters. That he wouldn't commit suicide, that he would handle his weapon better than a lot of the other shooters, and that he wouldn't be shot by the police because he would be finished before they could even react. He thought that Breivik's example was just what he needed to accomplish. No police came close to preventing Breivik while he performed his "cleansing of Norwegian society". Jack too would perform a cleansing. And it would not take elaborate planning. Just quick and efficient execution of a well laid out plan, the benefit of surprise as he saw in so many shooting sprees in the past would carry him through his

plot. And this is why he needed the M4 semi-automatic rifle, preferably an illegal one. He began actively plotting to carry out his attack late that fall, not long after his latest visit to his shooting club, only four months after he had met Conrad at the veterans get together. After he called the number on the announcements board at his club, he reached a thick voiced man who warily answered Jack. "I'm Jack McGee. I'm a member of Santa Ana Shooting range and club . I saw an announcement that was posted on the board there. Do you still have the item that you wanted to sell? "The man on the other end very reluctantly told Jack that he did still have such "an instrument" and that if he were interested maybe they could meet at the club on a pre-arranged date and they could discuss the terms. Jack immediately thought it was a mistake to give his actual name over the cell phone. He agreed to meet two weeks from then on a Sunday afternoon. He also said he wanted to try out the "instrument" before agreeing to buy. He thought it would cost him about $2,000. He didn't have that much money and he needed a couple more paychecks before he would have that kind of money. He would also need to buy ammunition, so he felt sure that for the next month or two he would have all his earnings accounted for.

In the interim Jack called Weedhead. Again Weedhead seemed not to remember Jack, but he made an appointment for him on a weekday evening around 8:30

four days away. When Jack got there, he was still unsure what he wanted tattooed, but he knew he wanted a big tattoo on his back, something related to his shooting skills. He had a hard time explaining to Weedhead what he was thinking of. Weedhead was also thinking of what could maximize his earnings and would be artistically interesting to him. It had been a warm day in spite of the gritty Santa Ana winds, and when Jack had come home from his work, he drank three beers. So he was feeling a bit light-headed when he got to Weedhead's and started negotiating a tattoo. It was always a little difficult understanding Weedhead, he half swallowed his beard and moustache when he talked and he had a funny accent. And as before it was busy in the small shop, the other two booths were occupied by equally chatty tattoo artists who seemed to be causing two girls some pain. After one of them squeaked, Weedhead winked at Jack and said, "They're both getting tattoos on their most sensitive private parts, if you know what I mean. Kinda like instruction manuals." and he chuckled. Finally Weedhead went to one of the walls and brought down a folder with various designs. "I have this really cool religious scene. It is Buddhist or Hindu or something or other like that. When I first saw it, it really blew my mind." He showed him the print. "You see, it's like a god giving illumination to the masses here below. They are figures with bursts of flame in place of heads, and the rays which emanate from this higher figure there, let's say it represents you, straight down at these masses of flame-heads, we could think of them as rifle shots in place of

transcendent grace or something or other. You see?" Jack did not know what transcendent meant. "And here, behind this superior figure's flame-head is an all seeing eye, like the masonic symbols which our Founding Father's put on the national seal. Isn't that cool?" It was definitely an interesting image. With rays spilling directly down from the superior creature, seemingly splashing into the flame heads of the assembled masses below him. It did look like a shooter shooting into a mass of people below. "Hey, that could do it." "Hey, man, I thought you might like. I've always liked this picture. I got it when I went to Thailand on an opium trip. It really blew my mind then. Just like all their devils and demons. Super scary, bug eyes, sharp teeth, everything. Just unreal. I can add some color to this in key places. You'll like it." Jack began to see himself in the higher figure with a flaming head. If his arms were brought together as if holding a rifle then this would be very much what he wanted. "Yeah, that could work. Can you do that now?" "Well you see it's already nine o'clock. I think, realistically this would take me about five hours to do. Lots of pin prinks will go into this one. I can keep it to three colors. So I would have to break this into two sessions, especially being as how I've worked my geezer off today. Maybe we can start now and I work for an hour or an hour and a half. And then you'll come back and I finish it on another evening, starting a little earlier. Whaddaya think?" "How much will it cost?" "I would say, around $400. But that would depend.

Can't think it would cost much more than that. Do you want it?" "Yeah, sure. Looks really cool, and unique. I think I can swing it, I mean the cost. Let's start." Weedhead started rocking his head forward and back, like he was a black actor from the 1970s or 80s. He directed Jack to take off his shirt andsit in the far booth, the comfortable one, and he took the image to the scanner. After it scanned he looked at it on the computer screen and then started to stretch and adjust it. He came over to Jack and began to measure his back. Then he stretched the computer image a bit more to fit it on the area he wanted on Jack's back. Jack could see it on the computer screen. It gave the figures a more other-worldly appearance, they were all dressed in robes with their arms up, receiving the grace or the bullets as the interpretation would have it. Then Weedhead added a palette and put daubs of orange and red here and there. It made the flameheads look like their heads were exploding. Finally he added a few red tear shaped imagines. "These are usually put in tattoos to indicate a number of kills." said Weedhead. "The gangsters like them. Like keeping score." Weedhead collected his needles, pots of dye, and some small rags, then he asked Jack to turn around and lean forward over a bar with his back to him. He would need to hold this position for over five hours while Weedhead put the image onto his back. Then the tattoo artist started. In spite of the alcohol, it seemed to Jack that Weedhead was working faster and pressing harder than usual and it hurt. Or maybe his back was more sensitive. After two hours, Weedhead pushed back, and said, "That's

enough for me for tonight." Jack saw that Weedhead's hair was wet and matted onto his forehead and down onto his cheeks. When Jack stood up, he couldn't believe how stiff and sore his back was. He needed a shot of something strong, whiskey or vodka, and a nickel bag of coke. But he did not have any money for any of this. He drove back home, tender and suffering, uncomfortable in his seat, wanting nothing more than the last two beers—weak stuff actually—that were still in the fridge. That would be his dinner for the night.

The appointed Sunday came and he put his pistol in a bag and got in his truck to drive out to the Santa Ana shooting club. He was driving along on the freeway to the east, when he noticed that a police car with strobing red lights was trailing him. He pulled over. It was a California Highway Patrol officer, that nemesis of speeders and dangerous drivers on California's highways. It was the first time in more than six years that Jack had been stopped. It must have been a routine stop on a late Sunday morning, but the patrolman almost immediately told him to show him his documents. "You know you're driving with Tennessee plates, and that they say 2008 as the date of the last inspection? How long have you lived in California?" "Officer, I guess it must be about six or more years, sir." The patrolman leaned over to look closer into the truck at Jack's face. "Are you Jackson Johnston McGee?" "Yes sir, that I am." "You know, you have to get your vehicle registered after you've lived in

California for six months?" "No sir, I didn't know that. I guess I just haven't gotten around to doing it." "Well you need to. And you need to get a California state driver's license, at the same time. You'll have to take the state driver's exam, because this license is out of state and has not been valid for five years here." "I'll do it this coming week. I promise." "I have to give you a summons. You can pay the fine to the county court, or you can choose to have a day in court as they can schedule it. What's your residence address?" The patrolman wrote out a ticket for him, walking slowly back to his squad car and taking his time. Jack could see him radioing in some information. Jack was going to be late and felt irritated by the patrolman's dilatory manner. Finally he came back up to his truck, handed him the summons and his license. Jack noticed that the fine was $400. "Your vehicle is not permitted to drive in the state of California and has been illegal for more than five years, that's why the fine is so high. I've notified the Highway Patrol central data and they've given you another week to drive while you get California registration plates. I suggest you get that done first thing Monday morning. I understand there are long lines at the motor vehicle offices. Have a good day." Jack was furious. He didn't have $400 to pay the fine, nor another $150 to get new plates. As it was he was going to be short of money to buy the M-4. He drove off and got to the club about 45 minutes late for his appointed meeting.

The club seemed abandoned when Jack arrived, even though there were four cars parked out front.

Everything was silent. There was nobody at the front reception area, not even the attendant, old man Cody, who usually sat at a counter on one side of the narrow foyer with his cowboy boots up on a bar in front of him. Jack had never been to the club when Cody wasn't there. And the small shop at one end of the foyer was shut and its lights were off. But Jack soon found the reason for the silence and the emptiness of the club: everyone was in the target shooting hall watching a contest, even old man Cody was there. There were two rows of elevated benches in the gallery behind the range and several people were seated there watching the targets displayed on large screens above two men standing next to each other on the central lanes with air rifles taking turns shooting at two targets at 25 meters. Jack sat down on one of the benches and watched. The contest moved slowly, each man taking his shot after carefully aiming for ten to fifteen seconds. After another six rounds and a close contest where both men were regularly hitting near on the bullseye, both men put down their rifles and shook hands. A tall powerfully built man in a red and blue checked flannel shirt had won the contest by a narrow margin. Old man Cody limped back to the front foyer along with the shop attendant. Jack decided it was time to call his appointment. He stepped back to the front of the foyer and called on his cell phone. The man answered, and said he was waiting for Jack and he would be in the foyer in one moment. The tall man in the red and blue checked shirt stepped into the foyer carrying his air rifle

in a carry-all. Jack introduced himself. “I watched you shooting just now. You’re a mighty fine shooter.” The tall man introduced himself as Sam Johnson and then said, “Yeah I used to shoot competitively for the army. Never good enough to make the Olympic team though.” Sam then invited Jack back to the lockers hall, which was a built out of heavy cinder blocks and had two steel doors at both ends. He opened a tall, double width locker and placed his carry-all inside and took out a leather bag. “Let’s go outside to the rifle target range.” Once there he put the bag on a table and opened it to reveal the M-4gerie in excellent condition. “I just don’t need this one anymore. I have several of them at my house. Enough to protect myself from zombies and blacks and other criminals. I want $1,300 for this beauty, made by Bushmaster. Maybe you would like to try out a few shots?” Jack agreed. He took it in his hands. Its heft seemed a little less than he remembered, but then they were light guns in general. He was relieved that Sam wanted so little for it. Sam handed him a short clip and Jack stood up to shoot standing at the target about 75 yards from the shooting line. The sight was clear and accurate, and he pulled off three clean shots dead on target before switching to automatic. Jack liked it and he decided to buy it. After his next paycheck in the coming week, he could afford to pay for it also. “I also was an army marksman. In Afghanistan. But I got into shooting by hunting for deer and boars. But I really like this carbine.” Sam did not ask Jack what he wanted the gun for, and he did not offer any commentary on Jack’s being in Afghanistan.

Jack and Sam agreed on a sale and that Jack would bring the full amount in cash the next weekend. Jack figured he had enough to get his new license and plates, to pay for this rifle and some ammunition, and to complete his new tattoo.

On Monday morning he asked his boss if he could take Wednesday off. He figured it would take all day to get his car registered and to get a new license. And in the late afternoon he could go to Weedhead. He also asked for an advance on his paycheck. The boss was a little annoyed by the two requests, but he relented and agreed to both in the end. As he expected he spent all day Wednesday from 8 am waiting in lines to get his new license and register his car. He found it offensive that so many of those waiting in lines in front of him were either Chicanos or blacks, and many of the remainder of petitioners were also foreigners, like Indians, Iranians or Chinese. None of the Chicanos seemed to be able to speak English, and as the day wore on his fury grew. Why were all these foreigners getting served in California? What were they doing there, when they could not even speak English? The longer he waited the more his fury grew. Not at the system, but at the other applicants. If he only had that M-4 right then, he would have sprayed the hall and killed every one of them, 'fucking foreign swine', he thought. He was ready to do this, because he had been reading about the white nationalists anger at the flood of foreign immigrants being encouraged and invited in by

"democrats and liberals" in Washington. This was the first time though that he saw in a pure distillation just what this wave of foreign immigrants really meant. At the very end of the day, he got his California driver's license, or at least the temporary license which he could use until the permanent one arrived later in the mail. (He had registered his truck earlier in the day and took his new plates and attached them to his truck there in the parking lot.) So by the time he arrived at Weedhead's salon, it was already past seven in the evening and he was hungry and irritable.

It seemed right from the smack that Weedhead was also in a foul mood. He yelled at one of his tattoo artists sitting in the next booth, he was slow to start on Jack, he dropped things, and he was not his usual chatty self. Instead he was muttering to himself over some incident that had happened earlier in the day. Once he got started he said half under his breath, "I could really use a reefer just now." He was not as concentrated as he usually was. And Jack paid for it on his back. The pinpricks were sharper and the pressure of each application was heavier. It was more painful than the first time when Weedhead started this tattoo. The work seemed interminable. It often felt as if Weedhead was sewing something onto his back, like a leather bib or something heavy, the pin pricks seemed to be pulling through his skin like stitches. Jack remembered the time when he had gone to an emergency dispensary and gotten six stitches for a knife wound to the thigh he had gotten by accidentally dropping an open whittling knife. He had watched as the nurse put in the stitches and he

had thought it felt strange when she pulled hard on the black thread and tightened each stitch. Of course he could not see what Weedhead was doing, but the sensations seemed the same in his memory. It was most painful for Jack as the pins applied their ink down above his kidneys down to the line with his undershorts. He did not suspect he was so sensitive down there. Twice, Weedhead took a breather and let Jack stand up and stretch. Finally after four hours, Weedhead pushed away and muttered, "Another masterpiece by the master, if I do say so myself. You can get up now Jack. Your canvas is finished. You might want to look at it in the mirror over there. Here's a hand mirror to help you see your back." Jack took the hand mirror and used it to look at the full length wall mirror which reflected his new tattoo on this bare back. It was impressive. It filled his back from between his shoulder blades down to his waist. At the top was a man standing on a hill of large rocks holding a large rifle and shooting down onto a cluster of people, backs to the viewer and with their arms upraised to the shooter as if worshipping him. All the people were featured with large flames in the place of heads. Weedhead had painted in the heads with orange and yellow ink. Straight lines, like rays of the sun, ran down from the shooter into the flame heads of the cluster of people, who were wearing long robes. These people were standing on rocks which Weedhead had painted at the very bottom of Jack's back, at the sacral curvature. In those rocks there were tiny serpents curled around the feet of some the people. The rays

emanating from the the shooter seemed to make small explosions into the flame heads, which Weedhead showed by adding red ink that looked like splashes. Behind the shooter as Weedhead had promised was a type of luminous aura behind the shooter's flame head, almost like the Masons' pyramidal eye of God. On the sides were swirls of clouds in blue, black and white ink, clouds which like in oriental paintings writhed and seemed alive. Jack liked this tattoo. He saw himself in the main role as the ascendant shooter. "Weedhead, you have really done something unique. You are a genius." It was already late, and both Jack and Weedhead were exhausted. Jack counted out four one hundred dollar bills and shook Weedhead's hand. "You really deserve this, this time." Weedhead said nothing. He started closing up the salon. As Jack opened the glass door to leave, Weedhead muttered, "Farewell, my friend. Carry my art with you carefully."

Jack had a rough night, with dreams of floating through the air, mass shootings down on people like the re-enactments he had seen of Breivik's Norwegian massacre, and the pain in his back interrupting his sleep causing him to flop and turn in the bed, or other dreams where he was trying futilely to shoot his rifle at onrushing Afghans who looked like black zombies, but when he shot only blanks would come out of his rifle and these dreaded mobs would overcome him. He was haunted by these dreams through the next day and into the next night as well. The rest of Jack's week was light. For some reason the garage had few cars to work on. Finally on Friday afternoon, the boss called Jack

over and gave him the check for his advance pay. It was enough to pay for his gun with a little left over to get him through to the end of the month. But there was not enough for even a small doze of crystal meth. He would still have to scrape to get by until the next paycheck.

That next weekend he went back out to the chaparral hillside where his shooting club was located. This time he arrived at the agreed time, no unanticipated stops by the Highway Patrol. Sam was waiting for him. "I suppose your having been in the army, you know how to use this fine weapon?" Sam asked as they went into the locker room. Jack grunted. "Sure I have used a very similar weapon to this one for my entire tour in Afghanistan, most of two years. It is great." It seemed Sam wanted to ask something else, but he gave it up. "The bag is mine, however." he said as he slipped the rifle out of the bag and handed it to Jack. He put the bag back in the locker. Jack put the gun on the table and pulled out his wallet to count out the money. As he was paying, he asked Sam, "Are you a member of the National Guard?" "No, I can't see any reason, in wasting more of my life in military service to the U.S. government, than I already did. You probably met lots of suckers who were in the National Guard and were sent over to Afghanistan or Iraq when the Defense Department desperately needed cannon fodder for their two wars. Why do you ask? Are you in the National Guard?" "No, I was just invited to join. It doesn't

seem like such a bargain." "It isn't. The idea was originally was to have a militia to protect citizens from the government, but instead the Guard has become another arm of the government's control over people." "Thanks, Sam." They shook hands. "Thank you. I'm not sure we'll see much of each other again. I'm going to stop coming here. Stay up at my ranch." Jack took the gun and a clip out to the outdoor rifle range and spent an hour getting accustomed to this gun shooting targets at 100 meters both in single shot and in rapid bursts. Then he wrapped the gun in a dark clothe and went out to his truck where he packed it under the rear seat, he got in and left. As he was driving the long dusty track down the canyon where the club was located, Jack felt a foreboding. He felt like he also would not ever be coming back to this club. He had had visions like this before. When he left Bagram in Afghanistan, he had a strong palpable feeling that he would never go back there. This time in his truck, very briefly, he wondered what had become of Kyle. He also thought what had become of his mother and father. By the time he drove up to his apartment compound, he was feeling depressed, as if someone was pressing hard in on his head.

In the following weeks, Jack spent less time on the porn websites and more time than before on the Breivik program. He became resolved that he could do the same thing as Breivik, only killing more people. He thought whether to shoot black people or Jews, but he couldn't actually decide. He knew the neighborhoods and towns in the surrounding region where blacks

predominately lived, and he read reports of towns that had high Jewish concentrations, but he could not figure out where in either case large numbers would congregate, short of a Lakers basketball game. But he wouldn't barge into a Lakers game—that would be too well protected, and as Breivik demonstrated it was better to go after a "soft" unprotected target and walk away than to go after a target crawling with guns and security forces. And besides, he was having some difficulty understanding whether or not he could get a police uniform. This issue caused him a lot of confusion and it pre-occupied him even at the garage. But maybe if he were to go on his shooting spree at night, it would not make any difference. He also could not figure out if he was going on his shooting spree to become a martyr or if he would walk away like Breivik did, a hero. But both at work and at home in the evenings, Jack was confused because he continued to feel depressed. He thought often about how his father and his mother never appreciated him or gave him much love and approval. He had over the previous months slowly stopped viewing porn sites and masturbating along with the videos. Not only did the sex sites no longer arouse him as much, he found that he was having trouble ejaculating. In the weeks following his purchase of his new M-4, he even began thinking about how, if he were to commit suicide, he would perform the act. He thought about shooting himself with his pistol through his mouth. He even had dreams about doing just this. But in his dreams

something always would go wrong, like there was a knock at the door, or the pistol would misfire and he had no bullets. He thought about driving his truck off the heights of one of LA's many freeway fly-overs. But there was also no guarantee that would kill him suddenly and finally. He did not want to end up in a hospital after an unsuccessful attempt to kill himself where other people worked to rescue him. At the garage, his boss discovered him once, lost as if in a trance because he was thinking about how he could get an effective, fast acting poison. Perhaps his depressions were worsened by the howling and heat of the Santa Ana winds at that time of the year, a time when dust seemed to creep into every crack, under the doors and windows, and the heat was oppressive.

At the end of the month he finally got the next paycheck so that he had the spare cash to buy a dime bag of coke. He took it home and snorted it. But the effect was not the euphoria of past years. There were dark lights, shooting pains which emanated from his shoulder wound, feelings of pressure first on his head, then his chest and heart, then in his crotch, and then on his head again. No visions of naked women, no erections, no sensations of sexual arousal and happiness, no flying around the ceiling. His breathing was tight and short. And then the pains changed to sensations that there were bugs crawling around inside him. First in his torso, then beetles climbing up under the skin of his legs. Then he thought he saw worms boring out of the figure and face of Annalyn lying stretched in his ventral tattoo. The next morning he

was suffering from intense thirst, which water did not seem to quench. And the headaches continued for several days afterwards.

One day while he was working on a transmission box, he recalled an event when he was only seven. He and Bobby had gone down to a schoolfield where a group of boys were collecting for a pick up game of tag football. Bobby was picked to captain one team and a boy aged eleven or twelve was picked to select the members of the other team. The two then selected from the group, nearly all of whom were ten or eleven and quite a bit bigger than Jack. Bobby picked Jack last, against the protests of the other boys who didn't want a little child on their team. Then they began to play, six a side. Jack stood out most of the game, but then when they had the ball in attack, after what seemed like a long time playing, Bobby called Jack to join the play. After the snap of the ball to Bobby who was playing quarterback, Jack was to run over the touch line and turn around and catch the pass Bobby would throw to him. Jack did just as he was told. No one paid him any attention as he was the littlest boy on the field. The ball came, it was not a long pass, maybe only ten yards, but it was coming toward him over his head. Jack jumped up with both his hands over his head. The ball struck right between his two hands and it felt heavy and abrasive, as if it would carry him away. But he grasped the ball hard and held on tight as he came back down to the ground, holding tight even as he fell onto his knees. He

had caught the pass! They had scored, they had won. Bobby rushed up to him shouting his amazement and approval, patting him on the back. Jack had done, just what Bobby had asked him to do, just what everyone was expecting he could not do. It was the happiest moment in Jack's young life, and ever after, he would remember fondly of the day he caught Bobby's pass and held on. And Bobby's proud statements of approval. He missed Bobby then. He began to cry over the transmission box, and when he was aware of it, he ran to the men's room to hide his shame. Only one other mechanic in the garage noticed that there was something wrong with Jack that day, but he could not tell what it was.

Finally Jack felt the time had come for his shooting attack. It was a Thursday evening. He had told his boss that he would not be coming in to work the next day because he was going to go to the VA. He took a swig of whisky with a small dinner. Then he took a stronger than usual dose of crystal meth after it had gotten dark. The high was amazing: shearing sounds and roaring like strong winds tearing through his apartment. Views of panels of color swam rapidly around the ceiling lamp. Small black and sometimes red spots fluttered in front of his eyes, or even through his eyes, like swift erratic fruit flies. His breathing was extremely fast, and he felt as if he were taking in too much air with each breath. His head throbbed intensely. And then the flame-head figure pulled off the tattoo on his back, stamping his feet on the floor, causing sparks to rise up. The flame head figure

grabbed Jack's rifle and pistol from the kitchen table and with yellow-orange words thrown straight into Jack's eyes, he roared. "Come on! Now's the time." Jack ran out of the room and out of his apartment, dressed in a black long sleeve shirt and black jeans and a pair of Converse sneakers without laces. It seemed Jack was walking about a foot off the ground. The flame-head figure was already in the truck and the two drove off, through the inky night along the highways of southeast Los Angeles, the street lamps shining like huge yellow dandelion seed heads. They drove down to the Dudley town Cine-Complex, and parked in the deep palm tree shade of the parking lot which was adjacent but more than 60 meters from the Cine Complex entrance. The pressure was growing intense. People looked at the two of them in fear as if they were giants floating angrily in the air to the Cine-Complex. They stormed in through the doors into a large blue and orange carpeted foyer. There were now screams at their appearance. A startled security guard, a paunchy black man in a sand colored uniform, nearly fell off his stool and started to react. But the flame-head figure drew out the pistol and shot him dead. Now people around them were ducking and trying to avoid them. A terrified teenager dropped a huge bucket of popcorn on the carpet and fled. They both flew into one of the cinema halls where there was a sign announcing the feature being shown, "No Country for Young Men". Inside, instead of the usual deep darkness and snugness, there was a huge brilliant bright, screen filled with a shining

desert landscapes and sun-burnt sky. In the middle of the screen was a giant mustachioed Mexican, outlined by a hot blue sky, shooting a shotgun straight into the audience and laughing wickedly. The Flame-Head Figure took out the rifle and began shooting at the Mexican in the screen, in semi-automatic mode. The seated figures in the velour padded seats reacted slowly, many just slumping over, many thought it was part of the screen entertainment and didn't react, and still for others seated in the auditorium it seemed their heads exploded. Then the screaming started again. Jack could not tell how long all this occurred, but he and the Flame Head Figure walked slowly it seemed down the corridor toward the screen, where the Mexican was cursing and swearing in English at his unseen victims. Finally they both turned around facing the auditorium with the full IMAX screen brightly shining behind them making them seem small silhouettes. The Flame Head Figure resumed shooting, shafts of light streaming down from his rifle in sharp straight lines like tracer bullets or shafts of inspirational light into the audience, which now was largely silent but at the same time the onscreen noise rose to a feverish level of keening, screaming and explosions. The movie kept rolling and its sound track was deafening. And then Jack walked over to the red lettered EXIT sign above the door next to the screen and he left, without either pistol or rifle. The steel doors of the auditorium slammed tightly shut behind him and immediately the screaming and turmoil inside the theater became muted. He walked slowly under the palm trees along concrete pathways set

between hedges of orange flowered plants. He calmly got back into his truck and drove slowly but deliberately away from Dudley Town Cine-Complex. Not even three minutes after he left the parking lot, as he was heading north on a wide well-lit boulevard, six police cars, their red and blue lights flashing and sirens screaming came rushing down the opposite side toward the Cine-Complex. Jack drove home, his rapid breathing slowed a little, his eyes hurting from the intense glare everywhere, and his back, the tattoo on his back, throbbing painfully. When he entered his apartment, to stop the pain, he tore off his shirt, and tried to apply some ice to his back. But of course he could not reach the source of the pains. He recalled that Weedhead had once said, “People don’t choose their tattoos as emblems they control, the tattoos choose their display surface, their hosts, and govern them.” He noticed a strange aroma, like lavender, permeated the apartment. Jack decided to take another dose of the crystal meth. “You’re a sonnabitch, Weedhead.” he angrily spoke out loud to himself. He looked in the fridge and saw a beer. He was so thirsty, so thirsty as if his mouth was desiccated from years of drought-- that he drank two cans before he went back to his usual plush chair.

After a wait of several months, Jamieson got a call from the County prosecutor’s office. A woman told him that

they had gotten a response to their legal appeal from the Defense Department's Bureau of Records. "I'll send the letter to you, but I thought you might want to know what is in the letter." "Yes, sure. Tell me." "It seems we got a favorable decision from them and they will tell us if they have a matching record of DNA belonging to a serviceman, either current or having served during the past 12 years when they started compiling these records. One matching to the DNA we submit to them. They are concerned that if the owner of this DNA is indeed a serial killer, that not only would withholding the information be an obstacle to achieving justice, but that it would also leave open the door to further killings." "So we can submit to them the DNA information we collected and they will tell us if they have a match to it. Right?" "Yes that's it. But as this is still part of the legal procedure started by the County Prosecutor, we'll have to submit the data from here." "That's fine." said Jamieson as he put down the handset in triumph. If this guy is still hanging around near here, he thought to himself, we'll get him now.

Another two weeks passed for the arrangements to be made and to get the response from the DNA database. But before they got the answer they were after, his office was called with news that the skeletal remains of another body had been found by a fire fighter –it was now late fall and with the hot dry weather, fires had begun on the chaparral—in a ravine in the Cleveland National Forest. Jamieson ordered a recovery team to get up there and collect the remains before the fire overran the area. Maybe this was a victim of the same

serial killer. But the bones when they were brought in and studied by the forensics team did not yield any new information. It was an older body, maybe it had been there for more than five years, and the bones which did not form a complete skeleton showed that they had been eaten by animals, perhaps a puma. But Jamieson still added this one to his list of missing females dumped in the scrub mountains of the western county. Finally he got the copy of the letter from the DNA database of the Defense Department. They confirmed that the sample of the DNA they had collected matched that of a veteran army soldier of the Afghan war who had been discharged nearly seven years ago. The soldier's name was Jackson Forrest McGee of Murpheysville, Tennessee. He had served with distinction two and a half years as a marksman private first class and as a mechanic. They had no further information on this individual. Jamieson jumped up. Now we know who we're looking for. He ordered that a wanted notification be sent out to all of the police organizations in California. Then he sent a request to the Bureau of Motor Vehicle Registration to find if this same Mr. McGee owned a registered truck in California. He then wrote up a similar request letter to the Tennessee department of motor vehicles to discover if there were any records of a truck registered to Mr. McGee of Murpheysville. He got back his answer from Tennessee first. There were indeed three registrations of such trucks it seemed. One was a four year old Dodge registered to Mr. Robert E. Lee McGee, one a

thirteen year old Chevy pick up to Robert Beauregard McGee, and a dark green Dodge Ram which was eleven years old to Mr. Jackson Forrest McGee, all registered to the same address. They seem to like Confederate generals in that family, Jamieson thought, because he was sure they were one family. He did not need to do much more investigating from the Tennessee side. The next day, he got the biggest breakthrough when the California Bureau of Motor Vehicle Records sent him information about the recent registration of a dark green, eleven year old Dodge Ram truck to one Mr. Jack F. McGee with his current address. Now things could start moving.

Jamieson submitted the request to the county prosecutor's office to obtain an arrest warrant and he notified his counterpart, Deputy Sheriff Lopez in the county of Los Angeles sheriff's department, a man he knew well, to get ready to make an arrest. But even before he got the warrant he asked Lopez to look at the McGee address and confirm if a dark green Dodge Ram truck was parked there and to begin surveillance of the address. When the warrant finally arrived, Jamieson called Lopez and arranged for an early morning raid on the apartment with heavily armed officers from the LA County sheriff's department. He explained to Lopez that the suspect was likely armed and a dangerous man. Jamieson asked if he and a deputy could join the arrest party.

The early Tuesday morning came when the police forces assembled around the apartment complex where

Jack's apartment was located. Two squads were located in the back of the complex and two advanced from the front sides. The time came. Eight heavily armed police officers, their hand guns drawn, and two others with battering rams at the ready stood on both sides of McGee's door. It was 5:45 am. Jamieson knocked loudly at the door. "Jack McGee. Open the door and come out slowly. It is the police." There was no reply for some minutes. Jamieson pounded again then gave the okay signal and the door came down with only the slightest of force. The apartment was dark and quiet as the police specialists rushed in and began to spread to the rooms. There was a nauseous smell in the apartment. Jamieson noticed a black shirt on the floor of the kitchenette and one large Converse sneaker by the door and one in the middle of the living room. One of the policeman signaled that there was someone in the bedroom. Jamieson entered the bedroom and snapped on the overhead light. "Jack McGee, get up! You're under arrest." But there was no reply and no movement. In the light of the bare bulb it could be seen that this was a dead body. There was dried congealed blood around the nostrils, and dried emesis by the mouth. There were flies on the body which flew up like a cloud when the police officers moved in to look more closely. The body was bare except for a pair of soiled boxer shorts. Jamieson was immediately struck by the tattoos on the back and front torso of the body. There was a pair of black jeans thrown on the floor. "This looks like the end of the line for our case. Search the

house for guns or ammunitions, or drugs." The LA inspector who had joined the arrest team in place of Officer Lopez muttered simply, "It looks like a drug overdose. We see lots of these all the time. Though maybe not with serial killers." 'Damnation.' thought Jamieson, 'we might never know whether he was our serial killer.' He looked in the jeans pocket and pulled out the recently issued California driver's license. "Jackson Forrest McGee. This is our man. But a dead narco is all we got." Jamieson looked closer at the tattoos. They seemed to have shriveled and grown older as Jack's body had dried. "I wonder how many days he has been here?" he said outloud to no one in particular. "Well look here, it must be less than a week, the flies' maggots are only just beginning to emerge from this tattoo of a naked woman. Disgusting." One of the police officers brought in a slightly crumped letter which was addressed to Jack. It was from the VA: a letter informing Jack that suicide was a major cause of death among young veterans and that if he had sentiments of feeling lonely, was desperate or depressed, or wanting to get out of this life then free counselling was available to him at a number of locations around the county. Jamieson turned again to the body and looked at Jack's face and then he noticed a small wirelike black tattoo that went clear round the neck. Maybe it looked like a thin line of barbed wire. On the Adam's apple over the line there were stenciled in black the small words, 'Cut Here'.

www.ingramcontent.com/pod-product-compliance
Ingram Content Group UK Ltd.
Pitfield, Milton Keynes, MK11 3LW, UK
UKHW040601210726
13854UKWH00008B/1667

9 781387 273126